PENGUIN BOOKS

THE RED VIRGIN

FERNANDO ARRABAL, a leading light of avant-garde theater since the late 1950s, is the author of several plays, including the classic *The Architect and the Emperor of Assyria*. He lives in Paris.

ANDREW HURLEY is professor of English at the University of Puerto Rico. His translated works include Fernando Arrabal's *The Compass-Stone* and Reinaldo Arenas's *The Palace of the White Skunks* (Penguin).

The
Red
Virgin

A Novel by

FERNANDO ARRABAL

—

Translated from
the French and Spanish by

ANDREW HURLEY

PENGUIN BOOKS

PENGUIN BOOKS
Published by the Penguin Group
Penguin Books USA Inc., 375 Hudson Street,
New York, New York 10014, U.S.A.
Penguin Books Ltd, 27 Wrights Lane,
London W8 5TZ, England
Penguin Books Australia Ltd, Ringwood,
Victoria, Australia
Penguin Books Canada Ltd, 10 Alcorn Avenue,
Toronto, Ontario, Canada M4V 3B2
Penguin Books (N.Z.) Ltd, 182–190 Wairau Road,
Auckland 10, New Zealand

Penguin Books Ltd, Registered Offices:
Harmondsworth, Middlesex, England

First published in Penguin Books 1993

1   3   5   7   9   10   8   6   4   2

Originally published in France as *La Vierge Rouge* by
Editions Acropole. © Editions Acropole, 1986.
Later published in Spain under the title
La Virgen Roja by Editorial Seix Barral, S.A.
© 1987 Editorial Seix Barral, S.A.

LIBRARY OF CONGRESS CATALOGING-IN-PUBLICATION DATA
Arrabal, Fernando.
[Vierge rouge. English]
The red virgin : a novel / by Fernando Arrabal ; translated
from the French and Spanish by Andrew Hurley.
p.   cm.
ISBN 0 14 01.7921 6
1. Mothers and daughters—Spain—Fiction.   I. Title.
PQ2601.R65V5413   1993
843'.914—dc20   93–20064

Printed in the United States of America
Set in Granjon
Designed by Lucy Albanese

YOU, YOU WILL RIDE YOUR STEED
IN THE SUNLIGHT . . .

The
Red
Virgin

1

TREMBLING IN EVERY FIBER OF MY BODY, I
write you.

How perfectly scrupulous I was with the police and the
judges, how stripped of all falsehood and dissembling, as I
told how I came to sacrifice you. Since that day, sole witness
to my own devastation, I have been racked by such terrible
torment! There is no pain I have not felt in my heart, no
grief I have not suffered. Was ever a woman so betrayed
by fortune!

How I feared throughout the trial that I would be found
insane! My attorney tried to make that monstrous lie the
capstone of his defense. How despicable it would have been
to subvert justice by employing a ruse so blatant! I detest
novels and stories of all kinds, for I am one who has never
lied in order to gain her own ends. And yet my attorney
dared to argue that only a deranged woman could murder

her own daughter. At once I stood up before the court, and with wisdom and firmness I restored the truth. It was so important that the world know the reasons for the sacrifice! Much more than my life was at stake.

I alone conceived you. Save for the indispensable assistance that was required to make your seed germinate within my womb, I worked alone. And, still alone, I exerted every ounce of my ingenuity and all my wits to devise ways to lead you down the paths of science, truth, and reality. Rightly did the world heap praise on you, calling you a prodigy in your earliest childhood, an astonishingly gifted young woman in later years, and then, at last, speaking the truth for all the world to hear, a supernatural wonder. And yet no one realized that you were much more than that, for your future promised heights yet unimagined. But just as the morning star was setting its kiss upon your cheek, you chose to hurl yourself into the abyss.

Now you, the messenger embodied, are no longer with me. No woman is a prophet in her own land. As I write you today, you dwell in a place so distant from this world! The envelope that held you has faded and eclipsed. Only your memory still burns and survives. How terribly I suffer! Through all those sixteen years of happiness (from 1919 to 1935), we obeyed, together, and with modesty and goodness, the laws of Nature. How happy we were!

2

ON THE SIXTH DAY OF JANUARY, 1918, EX-
actly one year before the day of your birth, I was dazzled
by a blinding burst of light which redeemed me from ignorance and ended the first passage of my life. I was in my
beloved father's library reading when there came, from no-
where, that flash of revelation. In how few years—for I was
but nineteen years of age—had I been made an old woman!
But that sudden bolt of revelation consumed the old woman
who weighed me down like a bale upon my shoulders, and
I was resurrected. Vanities, dreams, illusions, errors, my very
name, crumbled into dust. Like the Phoenix, I was born
again from those ashes, possessor of that personality that
you knew, ready to be happy and, infinitely more important,
filled with goodness. My life began with that mortal shock!

I departed my childhood swollen with the education
painstakingly imparted to me by my elders, through the

intermediary of my teachers. By those means my rebellious-
ness had been weeded out and I had been invested with
simplicity for my subsequent duties as a wife. In school I
was taught Sewing and Obedience; I learned to make chocolate pie and to feather the hard lines of my drawings; my
learning was sprinkled with notions about Arithmetic and
History and I was initiated into the mysteries of Embroidery
and Regional Dances. I never once kicked against the law.
How did *you* dare rebel against it, when you were no more
than an overgrown child?

I began to play the piano when I was eight; at nine, I
had learned the Marquess de Flamel's Rules of Education
by heart; and by the time I was ten I could produce lovely
calligraphic script, write a letter to the Governor, or curtsy
to a queen.

I was the second child of an intelligent, generous, understanding, upright, and good man. I never spoke to you
about him, yet I was his favorite daughter. Before I reached
twenty years of age I had discovered in his library the secret
books that transformed me. Even as I read the first pages
of the first volume, my admiration was drawn upward inexorably, to the very verge of ecstasy. I felt powerless to oppose
the dizzying magic, the infinite splendor of that work which
appeared to me more supernatural than human.

3

I DWELT EVER AFTER THAT MOMENT IN A world of hope, yet I saw my dreams fade as I told my beloved father of my plan. Seizing his attention on the wing, I announced to him without preamble or indirection that I wanted to be a mother—the mother, in fact, of an austere, brilliant, unique child, a child in whom Nature would repose her every grace, a son, or, better yet, a daughter who from the moment of her birth I might mold toward the realization of the Work. Wonder incarnate!

But my father behaved as though he were bereft of understanding and disillusioned of heart. He had eyes, but he could not see, or even guess, what it was that was enclosed at the heart of my plan. Saddened by my determination, he conceived the bizarre remedy of marrying me off.

How I have always striven to combat lies! He could not strangle my plan with the bonds of matrimony. From the first second my mind was set; I resolved to achieve my end by the most expeditious route.

My father's imagination wandered so far afield, into swamps of depravity, that it was soon muddied from its meanderings. What a grievous surprise that was to me! Vice, that scourge of humanity, inspired in me such disgust, such profound revulsion! How sorry I was not to have at my command a language even more measured and exact, so that I could make my father understand the essence of the plan that I would set in motion by giving birth to a living being!

I always pondered with my head, and not with my loins as so many men and women do. I had no intention of simply forging one link more in the chain of ignorance made up of uncouth slaves and inane enslaving teachers. That was why I would be a mother, and not some vulgar childbearer.

How shocked and scandalized my beloved father was when I told him that I was willing, ready even, to offer up my virginity! He could not understand, in spite of his goodness, the incomparable harmony a person such as I felt when I was in tune with my own conscience.

The plan filled me with joy; day and night I lived for it. And with what trust! Your birth would be but prelude to the astonishing destiny that would be yours as you lived your temporal life on earth.

I already loved you, and with such keen joy!

4

MY BELOVED FATHER WOULD SAY THAT MY reading was drying up my brain, that the time I spent in reading neither entertained nor profited me; it was all spoiled and wasted, according to him. He would speak to me affectionately and carefully, as though I were ill. He would take my hand and draw me under the wings of his solicitude, telling me over and over again that I was just a girl, that I was not even dry behind the ears yet, that the pointless yet poisonous ravings of those books, which were filled with lies and humbugs yet which I read so avidly and with such unrestrained excitement, were disordering my brain.

"You have become so odd!"

Long before you were born, I knew you would be a girl. I felt seized with such strange urges, such strange heat, such strange excitement! I sensed with such certainty that you would be everything that I, at this stage of my life, could no longer be.

My father tried to make me see a young man named Nicolas Trevisan. He was twenty-two years old, and he was recommended by his veneer of formality and his expectations: he had just finished his medical studies, and promised a fine practice. He had written me three letters, more sentimental maunderings than love letters, padded out with well-known verses.

My Aunt Sarah's garden was the seat of our rendezvous; tea, the dainty served. Meeting the young man, I might both obey my father and advance my plan. My aunt refused to leave us alone, not because she was concerned about my behavior but because she was afraid of what people might say.

"The neighbors are perfectly capable of taking you for something you're not and telling the world that you have no shame."

The night before our meeting, I dreamt of a little girl. She was flying through the air, and the colors from a prism illuminated her. She was sitting on the back of an eagle gliding solemnly through the sky. A constant, soft, endless breeze was wafting her toward the Sun, as though by a magic spell.

A few hours later, I dreamt that a man covered with scales was acting as guide for a young woman who had been blinded by the rays of the sun. In the air, a page or a messenger was fluttering around them, carrying a compass in his hand.

Then I heard a woman's voice say to me: "I feel filled with knowledge, riches, and health."

5

I PASSED THE SEASON THAT PRECEDED YOUR birth going out at night dressed in castoffs I had found in the attic. One night I was wandering through the back streets by the docks, seeking the path to my plan, when I came upon Chevalier, a man who, upon his own path, was wandering from perdition to perdition.

He smiled as he approached me.

"Are you searching for a man with your little light?"

As I was not carrying a light, his question disconcerted me. But I, like Diogenes, told him the truth, that in fact I *was* searching for a man.

Chevalier laughed so delightedly!

"You too? Poor little woman!"

No one had ever bestowed such a title on me. How ill it sat with me! It made me feel like reducing him to a "poor little fellow."

"Do not grow angry, my ladyship, at my lightning bolts of dung."

His manner of speaking was so odd that I took him for a follower of the cult of paradox. His mind was enlightened by the sputtering sparks of madness more than by the light of reason.

"I am the consolation of the disconsolate."

He cried out mystifications at the top of his lungs, he shouted counsel and advice as though he were indeed, in his own words, the Hospitaler of the poor and bereft. But his own miseries and misfortunes, no one could succor, much less stanch the lifeblood that flowed from them. So many years we spent together, shoulder to shoulder, amassing memories and accumulating stocks of nostalgia!

In truth, Chevalier scattered his charity less like a consoler of the wretched than like some inviolable living asylum for the persecuted and downtrodden. His chimeras were rooted in absurdity and capriciousness. His inexactness confused me; he spoke haltingly, in gushes and spurts, never hitting upon the *mot juste, simple et pleine*, which is what has always commanded my own admiration.

"I am an enchanted butterfly and, sometimes, a bumblebee with poisoned sting."

We parted at daybreak. Then, as I was beginning to fall asleep, he tossed a pebble at my window.

"Come down, and crawl into the wine vat with me."

6

WITH SERENE AND UNCONCEALED TENDER-
ness I would sometimes talk to stones, and sometimes I
would question them about all things divine and human.
All that separated me from your birth was the brief shock
of the conception; but how hermetic I became for those who
heard me speak, in spite of my passion for exactness! My
language would grow twisted and distorted, as though however hard I tried to communicate my thought, I could never
finally make myself understood.

How agitated my aunt grew as the hour approached
when I would meet Nicolas Trevisan in her garden! She
refused to let me trample upon my father's instructions and
be alone with him. My insistence distressed her terribly, but
my determination at last made her yield.

Self-trust led me direct to the truth. In the path of certainty there was no place for turning aside, nor for going

off wandering through the wide labyrinth of the imagination.

Nicolas had nothing more to say to me than he had already set down in his letters. He overloudly proclaimed again that he was in love. Thus I felt strengthened in my belief that there is no such thing as chance or coincidence, for all things are foreseen and foreordained. Neither he nor I could alter the inalterable will of destiny.

Looking at him fixedly, I told him that I abhorred and despised all that Vice clutched in its tentacles. He stared at me in bewilderment and confusion, and his expression lost its grandeur, nobility, and beauty.

I took advantage of this moment to reconcile the irreconcilable. I attempted to untangle that misunderstanding, although nothing bound me to his life, much less to his ways. But it might be thanks to Nicolas that my body, in its wisdom, could procure for me the sign and the seed necessary for your birth.

"I am at the perfect moment of my cycle. My period ended ten days ago. And my menstruation comes with perfect regularity."

For a few moments, after I had unveiled to him the outlines of my plan, I enjoyed a mood of such gentleness, a spirit of such softness and balm!

7

IT WAS WITH NICOLAS TREVISAN THAT I UN-
dertook my first aborted attempt to become a mother.

My sister, Lulú, had left among our neighbors a very bad
memory, and an even worse reputation. She flew off to New
York City as she breezed through life, forgetting that one
of her flirtations had unexpectedly left her with a child. A
brazen couple named Otero had received her into their crew
of nocturnal revelers. She spent her evenings with them in
famous restaurants and in anonymous bars. "Miss" Otero
was an over-the-hill ballerina some quarter of a century
older than Lulú and with less than half her advantages.
How horrified I was whenever I was compared with Lulú!
My sister was a creature so repugnant and so filled with
carnality!

I thought it wise, and also thought the moment right, to
detail to Nicolas Trevisan my anatomical character, gyne-

cological state, and endocrinological comportment. With what surprise he stared at me! He was thinking no doubt of my sister, but the spider that wove the threads of my nature was my own, not hers.

Avoiding the light of day, Lulú lived at night, like some rose at the Far Northern Pole. The stories of her pregnancies, her wanderings, her slips and falls fed upon themselves and grew fat as they passed from lip to lip. What a creature of the shadows she became as she willfully fled perfection! That is why I explained, ever so calmly and quietly, my plan to Nicolas Trevisan:

"I want us to couple, but without pleasure, or desire, or passion."

I thus spoke aloud for the first time the preface to my plan. I took advantage of his silence to praise you. How different you would be from the creatures that throng the earth! You would embody energy, and virtue, and herald the good tidings.

Nicolas, paralyzed by stupefaction, looked incredulously at me. I calmed him with my sentiments and my truth. I never aimed for any other end or harbored any other hope than the realization of my plan, nor could anyone besmirch my disinterestedness.

"The Fire will be extinguished when the Work is wholly consummated."

8

AS MANY HIDDEN AND SECRET HOLLOWS
riddled the spirit as hidden stars the firmament. Nicolas
Trevisan bubbled and sputtered in agitation, his expression
melancholy, his features baffled, his eyes bizarrely blinking.

"I am convinced you don't know what you are saying.
My love for you is spiritual, only spiritual."

With that stinging reply he gave me to understand that
there was only the slightest breath of separation between
Lulú and myself. My sister danced with depraved aristocrats
and howled—so crudely!—when she laughed. She had gone
off so heedlessly to live in New York, without a backward
glance toward Benjamin, the son she had abandoned. I
pushed aside wet nurses, nannies, and sitters and I took
charge of him, with heart and hand. But the government
at last, years later, took him away, charging that simply

because I myself was a minor, I lacked the discernment and maturity necessary to care for him.

The plundering and pillaging she wrought upon herself physically degraded Lulú, and so vulgarly! Nor did she manifest respect for the little her self-vandalism had left intact. Before her vices had carved their furrows in her features her beauty had been ethereal, filled with grace. And yet others saw her decadence as splendor. When first she went to New York, at nineteen years of age, she could only mimic others' gestures; she dressed gracelessly and without taste, she made decisions without serious analysis, she acted without real character, and she copied rather than develop her own creativity. How voluptuously she embraced falsehood! What a different world I lived in!

Opening my arms to faith and cultivating modesty, I made certain that my attitudes and my words remained obedient to my ideas, and that is why I sincerely and forthrightly revealed to Nicolas Trevisan my plan:

"I am not talking about love. I am proposing that you undertake a unique enterprise, one which, should it come to fruition, will honor your entire life: I want you to be the father of my future daughter."

Nicolas Trevisan could not understand my words, and so he sought out nests and cabins in which he fancied my riotous appetites and my insistent passions might be slaked.

"Do you want to marry me . . . or what?"

I dreamt that the Sun and the Moon were bathing in that original liquid composed of the nectar of the Seed. The outward fire of Sulfur dissolved, sublimated, and at last calcined the liquid, transforming it into Mercury.

9

I REALIZED THAT FROM THE BEGINNINGS OF eternity itself, before you were ever conceived, you already existed. You preceded the gushing forth of the pristine fountains of the earth, the shadows of the first clouds of the sky. You had existed forever, even before your spirit's body had divided itself into members. That was an obvious fact, and I grasped it from the moment I conceived the plan. I told Nicolas Trevisan the whole truth:

"I have no desire to marry you, I want to be a mother. I wish to couple with you only for the precise time necessary to be made pregnant. The fruit of that momentary carnal act will bring the project to consummation in its due time. I have prepared myself for that sublime future with deliberation, wisdom, and energy. My daughter will be the symbolic honey, the gate of heaven, the dwelling place of knowledge, the palm of patience, the mystical rose, the flower amid the thorns, the spiritual vessel. She will bring to pass all that I have been unable to accomplish for lack of education, training, upbringing, and time. The revelation came so late to me that I shall never now be able to gain that new world. I shall take pains without rest so that her education and upbringing will lack for nothing."

Stripped of the unreal symbolic veil with which his expectations had invested me, I appeared to Nicolas Trevisan's eyes the very personification of substance. How he trembled in fright and dismay! He stood up from the garden bench on which we were seated and gazed at me like an old man, defeated, peering anxiously through the fog all about him. Disturbed, mute, he helplessly contemplated the ungraspable wonder.

"What are you talking about? I am convinced that you do not understand the import of your words."

He feared that what had begun as a moment of tolerated, yea permitted, recreation would fall into repugnant vice. But the stuff of life always surrenders to the urgings of the spirit. Once more I explained it all to him:

"If the word is made flesh in order to live among us, the flesh may become word in order to come forth in my womb. I ask of you only that you penetrate my flesh for a few moments with your flesh, so that you may deposit within me the drops of liquid that my project requires."

10

NICOLAS TREVISAN TOOK ON IN MY PRESENCE
the blush of a man bewildered; he settled his hat on his
head like some automaton in the shape of a gentleman, and
he said:

"I must go. I have another appointment. I had forgotten."

He showed extreme emotion, he perspired in bafflement,
his faculties were surprisingly agitated. He bent stiffly from
the waist, while his chest and his face thrust forward. His
hands, moments before petrified, now took on life. He
trembled.

"Do I frighten you?"

The young man suddenly grown aged had made the
decision to cut short a situation which he found wonderful
and terrible.

"Forgive me. I must go."

I asked him whether it was my plan that so disturbed him.

"Goodbye!"

He clicked his heels like an officer, stood a moment at attention, bowed almost imperceptibly, and walked away so suddenly that his steps soon turned to flight.

After this first disappointment, my plan stumbled over other obstacles of much the same sort.

The essence of my plan I judged unworkable. It provoked revulsion in the candidates for its realization, who invariably turned accusers. Reason banged its head against the impenetrable wall of their convictions. How they fled my presence! For some, I seemed to have emerged from Chaos mad, dark, and shadowy, my very presence embodying confusion; for others, who stood at the verge of a flaming abyss, I appeared shameless, brazen, amoral. My physical aspect mattered less to them than my virtues. Torn between arguments and perverse appetites, they were at last defeated and captured by fear.

That night I dreamt that a little girl became first a mermaid and then a nymph crowned with long, sharp needles. She was swimming in the ocean through shoals of sharks, and from her breasts two streams of white liquid trickled into the waves.

11

THROUGH EVERY STAGE OF HIS LIFE CHEVA-
lier wore his true face. He would come to visit me at night,
tossing a pebble against my window as he had that first
night; then he would wait in the street for me to put my
head out. Together we would walk the streets until the first
light of dawn began to streak the sky, and I would never
find any reason for disgust at his nonsensical ideas and
outrageous words.

Chevalier had no respect for truth or for anything else;
he had no pretensions to profound virtues nor did he descend
to the pettiness of subtlety and dissembling. He spoke in a
language that ought to have irritated me as much as my
own ought to have irritated him. How seriously he would
utter phrases that to my mind made no sense whatever:

"The whinnying of seabirds makes me shiver."

"My guts are gorged full of knives and horror."

"I am a mad vagabond damned to live among cheap tin
swans."

He often sprinkled his conversation, without rhyme or reason, with words whose meanings did not jibe at all with his fantasies:

"Like a sheet-metal shark, I am bitten in the silence by Proteaceae."

Chevalier would bestow the most terrible obscenities upon drunken sailors without one moment's concern for my opinion. And yet he liked to hear me talk, in spite of the fact that he called me a conceited pedant and a know-it-all. But how delightedly he would listen to me when I rambled on about you! Even before you were born, how I spoiled you! With hundreds of curious questions he took my plan apart into tiny pieces—as though he could decipher the project! Without the slightest shadow of faith he penetrated the heart of the sanctuary; he often wandered down false paths, but his pleasure, contagious, constantly burst out. How excited it made him to tell me about his own adventures!

"Do you know Bardón, the toreador? As priggish and hoity-toity as you are, I suppose not."

What an enigma his life was. Even when he told me, in a disgusting lavishness of detail, about his repulsive adventures, I could not be offended.

"I have wandered heaven and hell with my little brass stars all a-tinkle. How delicious it was when we embraced! I could smell the mud of his legs and I heard the cool essence of the nuptial chant. Suddenly, as I had him at the peak of his swoon, and to the sound of muted horns, I bit his pigtail."

The esoteric lore of love took shape for Chevalier in an arbitrary set of abject gestures. That is why his words did not sting me, although they did, rightly, and to a terrible extent, horrify my conscience.

12

MY BELOVED FATHER, ALL MY CARE AND VIG-
ilance notwithstanding, died ten months before you came
forth into life. His legacy was parceled out according to the
paragraphs and clauses of the will, which bore strong traces
of his soul. Lulú did not come to claim what our father had
left to her; the attorney sent her portion, contained in a
voluminous diplomatic pouch bulging at the seams, to the
consulate in New York.

Benjamin sent a telegram from London, where he was
conducting a concert. He had, at that time, not yet celebrated
his twelfth birthday, but it seemed an eternity to me since
he had been abducted by the authorities. During those long
months he lived at the Conservatory, we wrote each other
every day. When his international tours as a pianist began,
our correspondence waned. Then came his triumphs as con-
ductor, and silence.

That telegram, how many memories it unleashed! Into the terrible grief brought me by the death of my beloved father there was braided an infinite nostalgia. I thought I had forgotten Benjamin, but once again his memory rushed over me, before I realized. Once more I felt the frustration that had choked me when the government carried him off to the Conservatory. That terrible disappointment, which I thought long dead and buried, fermented yet, with nauseating acidity, and reeking of the tomb.

My father's passing brought me suffering so painful that it was as though I were bound hand and foot and lashed with grief. Death had caught me so by surprise! And yet I had always considered it a sign of the regular, efficient working of Nature. The knowledge that I would never again see my beloved father was a wound so deep, so toxic, putrid, and infected, so resistant to any cure!—a grief not perceptible to the sense of smell but only to one's reason.

I did not abandon myself to grief, however, and much less to desperation. I had to set you up in the world, disarm curses so that you would never know grief, disappointment, or dejection.

Most of my life, whether in the alleys of my agitations or on the avenues of my prostrations, I have spent thinking of nothing else but you! My sacrifices were always free of any contamination of improper self-interest.

13

DURING THE DAYS THAT FOLLOWED THE
death of my beloved father, Chevalier, quite discreetly, set
out to counsel and console me. The advice he gave derived
from his own arbitrary interpretation of my grief, but his
attempts at consolation served me as apology and as en-
couragement. How absolutely I had surrendered to despond-
ency and dejection!

I had loved my father very much for his goodness and
his generosity. His lack of sagacity mattered very little to
me, for his intellect always gave true and indisputable proof
of his integrity. My mother publicly deceived him; a little
while before my father's death, she shared her lover with
Lulú. Each one, in turn, took her pleasure with Benjamin's
father, in frank mockery of the blame and vituperation of
their family and those closest to them.

Lulú and my mother went from cabaret to cabaret, insensible to the claims of goodness or of charity. For them, purity lay motionless and insipid, hidden and inert. Only frivolous and serpentine excitement made their eyes light up. They were drawn to biting, caustic falsehood; they caressed it, ceaselessly, and it was like some poisonous domestic worm whose venom pitted and corroded everything.

My mother was crowned with a full, flaming head of hair. You would be so different, so much the opposite of those two! How exhaustedly my father watched the deceitful, riotous license of his wife.

"She is a salamander that lives upon fire and feeds itself upon living coals."

I saw Lulú as an incombustible lizard. The two women retained their own natures, even when they consigned to the fires of their passions what they should have held most sacred. That perhaps is why they hated each other with such searing rage. When Lulú ran off to New York, my mother refused to let us accept Benjamin's presence in our house. How she insisted that he be sent to the Orphanage!

And then when I least expected it, Benjamin changed my life. I was thirteen and he was four when I began to teach him Music. That event acted as a life-giving spark, by which Energy was communicated to lifeless Matter. Until that instant both my essence and my substance were hidden, dark, frigid, and unformed.

How my father loved Benjamin!—though with a love so different from my own. But he could never bring himself to resolve the mystery of his presence among us.

14

CHEVALIER NEVER MET MY MOTHER, OR LULÚ, or Benjamin. These last two had already left the picture when Chevalier burst so suddenly in upon my life.

"I imagine your sister and your mother, from what you say, as inhabiting a world of cloudbursts and Roman-candle sparks, natural springs and ashes, roots and locomotives, and weighed down with gloom and envy."

How difficult I found it to understand the exact meaning of Chevalier's sentences! But perhaps not even he himself could follow the thread of his words. I suspected that for Chevalier the three of them—Benjamin, Lulú, and my mother—formed a trinity, a group more complementary than heterogeneous.

How lovingly my father would always offer me his counsel. My life revolved around him, while Lulú was caught in the vortex of my mother's gravitation. Those two women took such pleasure in satisfying their evil instincts and their fits of cowardice! They were incapable of telling the truth if standing up to falsehood put their well-being in danger.

My father was so different! He was an absolute devotee of the cult of a man's word, of sincerity, of honor. From the time I could read and write, tell right from wrong, he allowed me to read any book in his library. He would say that I would at least learn rigor from them. Sitting beside him reading, what intense and unforgettable hours I spent! I glimpsed within certain books, under their veil of stirring plot, a naked truth. Three months before your conception, I read that pure, frank, white, innocent book that renewed me spiritually and guided me to beatitude. The wise author imbued me, page by page, and without the least unctuousness, with the astonishingly limpid, precisely pure, and oh so simple Magisterium.

My sister preferred to wander among dark shadows, clouds, and complications. She behaved like some female devotee of primitive Chaos, which she, out of blindness, called "passion." How mercilessly she subjected her body, with no respect for herself whatever, to aberrancies, fits, and uncouthnesses!

One night when she was but thirteen, though already terribly wasted and worn by her unbridled descents into dissipation and debauche, she came home so late that my father said to me:

"One day you will learn that the Seed of the Earth is folded with Night into the Sand of the Desert, in a triple symbol of Death."

15

"WHEN I TELL THEM MY PLAN, THEY RUN.
Why don't *you* help me to become a mother?"

Shattering my illusions, Chevalier looked at me in shock;
he knew that his flesh could not profoundly affect my body.

"You would be the ideal collaborator in helping me to
mark a change in my state."

He replied with one of those verbal convolutions that
sounded so pretty to my ears but that my intellect had so
difficult a time in disentangling.

"You want us to have carnal knowledge of one another
on a narrow bed of stone as long as an ocean liner and
surrounded by the languid archangels of our dreams?"

"All I want you to do is deposit in my womb a few drops
of your sperm."

"My poor shipwrecked sailor raises his scimitar and unleashes his fury only when assailing the hairy body of a man."

"I ask for neither your affection nor your love; I ask only for your collaboration for a few moments so that I can bring my body to parturition."

"How you talk! You know very well I have great affection for you! I love you with dew-drenched lilies, as though you were my little sister with eyes of night. When I catch sight of you, it is as though I were watching you fly to me through trees hung with stars. But you must not ask of me what I cannot give."

"You aren't taking me seriously!"

"Of course I am! But you possess a silhouette too formal, too austere. You are attempting to escape a difficult situation by being so sensible! so solemn! so movingly priggish and pedantic! You talk like some musty university professor. You're neither fish nor fowl."

Chevalier, even with the scant light that burned in his untutored brain, could send me off daydreaming. In the blink of an eye he would leap from the ranks of the profane to the circle of the hermetic Initiates, as though he had been spiritually renewed. Without a thought he would turn into one of the Blessed or, contrariwise, refusing to be regenerated, would spurn all spirituality and simplicity. His mind, indolent yet boldly impetuous, pulled him about hither and yon, and he felt more comfortable, more "at home," with himself than with another.

But Chevalier, too, refused to become your father.

16

STILL STUNG BY THE REBUFFS I HAD RE-
ceived, I remarked to Chevalier that he did not understand me.

"Of course I understand you! I'd love to be a mother
too, and feel my belly swell with waves and jingling bells.
How swept away by joy I would be if I could see a magnolia
of blood, bellowing like a furious little bull, emerge from
my womb, between my masculine thighs. How wonderful
to be a woman!"

With growing delectation, he already began to feel himself a mother, if vicariously. I would sometimes wonder
whether he was not awaiting your birth with greater nervousness and happy expectancy than I myself. My mind
made up to respect the philosophical doctrine of my plan,
"philosophical" taken in its traditional meaning, I would
assume the straightforward role of unadulterated theorist

when I talked with Chevalier, but he, crumbling under his need for facile directness, preferred the blazing torches of practice to the tentative light of speculation.

"When are you going to discover the difference between appearance and reality?"

In the conflicts that arose after the death of my beloved father, Chevalier strengthened my resolve with his prudent counsels, which were the fruits of his lack of respect for both divine law and human scripture. The attorney tried to stall my access to the inheritance as long as he could. The capital left by my father, together with the income from certain properties, would allow me to carry out the external part of my plan without want or financial need. After Lulú collected her portion of the inheritance at the consulate in New York, we never heard from her again; it was as though she had been swallowed up in two great gulps by her gluttonous suitors.

A short time before his death, my father recounted to me an episode from my childhood that I had completely forgotten. When I was a very little girl I had a doll I was mad about, a doll that would walk a few steps if you wound her up. One day I asked why she wouldn't just walk by herself, without having to be set in motion by one of us. One of the maids replied that my doll was not alive. To the apparent liking of very few, and to the special grief of my father, I replied:

"One day I'll have a *real* doll of flesh and blood."

17

HOW CHEVALIER LOVED THE PHOTOGRAPHS
of Benjamin and me at the piano, playing four-hand pieces!
These photos had been pasted in the last pages of my beloved
father's album.

When Benjamin was abandoned by Lulú, someone from
the Maternity Hospital brought him home. I recall that for
the first few months his tantrums at night would unleash
my mother's fury, without lessening the abhorrence her
daughter inspired in her.

"He's going to be just like Lulú, Satan's brood."

At first I looked upon him as an ill-come interloper. My
father's passion for that constantly demanding, crying creature was a very unpleasant surprise for me. When he came
home from his office in the evening, my father would rush
to that strange intruder's crib even before he took off his
hat; he would make faces at the baby and coo in the most

unembarrassed way to get its attention. He would give orders and make suggestions, so that the baby might grow up big and healthy. When the child fell ill, my father would stop going to his Club; he would sit at the head of the crib the whole night long.

My mother, one night, brought from its shadows, out into the light, the knotted imbroglio:

"The child's father is the captain of the *Moratín*. That tramp Lulú got herself involved with him. Doesn't it disgust you that the fruit of that sickening union is living under our roof? Its place is in the Orphanage. When are you going to send it off once and for all?"

"I thought that the captain was *your* lover."

My father felt no disgust whatever at loving, with all his heart, a child that had been born out of the intrigue between his wife's lover and his own daughter. But I! What revulsion I felt, hearing from my mother's very mouth the confirmation of so much of the servants' gossip! What a harsh burden of misery!

I dreamt of a woman who rode a horse into a temple where she lay a madrigal at the feet of her beloved, while an elephant with a tower upon its back floated in the air.

18

I NOTED THAT CHEVALIER SPOKE CLEARLY only when, washed by a clear and bubbling tide of austere emotions, he attempted to rise above or spurn his profane ones. One had to be there to hear him talk to a carabinero! He expressed himself with such clarity and precision that one would have sworn he was an open book. To me, however, he said, with as much haughtiness as ingenuousness:

"What ideas you have! Be radiant! Flutter like a mechanical grasshopper in the midst of mirrors and melancholies."

I possessed neither his double language nor his scraps and tatters of doctrine. How arduous, for me, appeared the simple task of your conception!

And yet I was already knitting the mantle of your future education. How devotedly I would keep alive the flame of reflection and discernment, without ever allowing you to stray from natural simplicity. I calculated precisely how much rest and nourishment would be needed to foster the regeneration of the old cells of your body and those that would be worn away by daily labors. I thought of myself as architect and planner, and I refreshed my imagination with a rainshower of conjectures.

How often I would wake at dawn to work on the plans for your life!

You would learn to extract light, to guide it across the surface of things until you had achieved true sublimation. You would accomplish everything, thanks to Science and goodness. I already called you "my idolized daughter."

It was inconceivable to me that you would be born a boy. How racked by impatience I lived!

Joshua had to march around Jericho seven times before the walls of the city fell, upon the eighth. The swans also circled Delos seven times, and Apollo was born as they completed the eighth. And I, I wondered, which revolution was I now making? And how many rebuffs would I have to suffer before I found your progenitor?

Those defeats never, though, made me lose hope. I was ready to meet my destiny and yours with wisdom and to interpret those destinies with calm good sense.

I hit upon the excellent decision to trust in myself, and this was the essential piece in the construction of my project.

19

WHEN BENJAMIN, GROANING AT INTERVALS, would suffer migraine headaches, my father would massage his temples with infinite patience, while my mother, with more repugnance than sarcasm, would, under her breath, hurl the rough stones of her mockery at the suffering boy.

How graciously and tenderly my beloved father would knead the painful places! His fingers and his soul combined to set the flesh right again and to draw out the pain his grandson was suffering. And now, reminded by that, I would daydream about your health. Thanks to the complete and perfectly achieved education which you would receive from the very cradle on, you would possess the triple gift of wisdom, good fortune, and felicity. You would be the mirror in which all humankind would see itself reflected.

"But what nonsense! Stop daydreaming about that

daughter of yours! Abandon yourself to an ocean illuminated by mint-scented candles."

Chevalier would concoct artifices by which to proclaim his vapidities when he pretended not to understand.

"My daughter's life will be lived in the shelter of Nature's masterpiece: the Tree of Life."

"I see—when you go off to scour the countryside it's a sign that you've been jilted again."

"Human industry cannot help me."

"Does that mean men run away like skittish colts?"

"The moment I tell them, straight out, what it is I want of them, they seem shocked, and run off blushing."

"There are no real men left. They all died in the nineteenth century. All that's left are butterflies with monocles."

"This afternoon I saw the lawyer's son I told you about. The one who seems to want to court me. As soon as I found myself alone with him, I told him I had prepared myself, that I had bathed, and that I was at the ideal moment, the perfect time of my period. The second I asked him to take carnal possession of me, he leapt up and ran off like a shot, as though I had spat on him."

"There are no fighting cocks, or dusty throats, or galleons of war, or conquered loins, or thick hot roots—there are only oafs and addlepates."

20

AFTER THE DEATH OF MY BELOVED FATHER,
Chevalier would come often to my house, without the least
fear or embarrassment. We would play the four-hand piano,
as I had with Benjamin.

From his third birthday on, Benjamin came, quite eagerly, under my complete custody and care. When, against
his every inclination and desire, he was taken away to the
Conservatory, he was eight. He had never set foot on the
grounds of any public school or the dais of any private
academy; it had been I who had persuaded the child to savor
the sweet taste of knowledge, who had taught him to read
and to write and above all to play the piano. But how many
mistakes I made! And how serious they were! Zeal and
exultation so clouded my emotions that at last they clouded
my faculties as well. But with you, I was convinced, my
physical emotions would not render me unfit for my work.

My father knew that Benjamin played the piano wonderfully well for his age. One evening, the proud grandfather, he took him with him to his Club, with the idea of dazzling his friends. And indeed they were so amazed that they took Benjamin, more slave than free, to the Conservatory, where he gave a triumphant recital. There was no longer any way to rescue or to ransom him; Lulú signed the documents necessary for the State to take charge of him and to be his only tutor. Soon his tours began, under the strict control of a professor from the Conservatory who had usurped my place.

Those dramatic events took place when I was but seventeen years old; suddenly I felt so old, so freezing cold, so bent and wizened, so disillusioned, disappointed, and spent!

I dreamt, during that time, that an entire faculty of female professors had locked me into a stone coffin to punish me for my illnesses. A pack of smiling squirrels came to gnaw at my flesh and my bones.

How those memories grieved me, futilely, for years and years, until you were at last born! I passed through an embryonic stage, a winter that lasted years, during which the buried Seeds underwent moist fermentation. But in the mountains, there was the thunder that announced the hour of rebirth. How eagerly I awaited the appearance of your progenitor!

21

CHEVALIER LIVED WITH A FRIEND OF HIS, A man of advanced age and declining health, named Abelardo.

"He is tall, bald, and consumptive. He also has infinite patience, and he will hold things against one for an eternity. He sits and waits for me day and night, like a Trappist monk."

How Chevalier would have rejoiced had he had the power to bestow life upon dead dross and health upon his friend.

"I am on the watch for the black cloacal well hidden under his confounded consumption, so that I can dry it up."

He thought he could attract, seduce, and swallow up Abelardo's disease. For Chevalier, though, morality was a stranger as unfamiliar as was fidelity. He perched himself at a height where vice, falsehood, and fantasy reigned in solitary splendor.

He would recount to me, quite openly, the most lascivious acts of shamelessness and the most dissipated indecencies, in the most shocking and scandalous words.

"Last night I had a rendezvous with a fiftyish puritan with holy medallions, a hymnbook, eyes made out of rags, and moth-eaten hopes. I give English lessons to his son. The moment he laid eyes on me, a week ago, a rage began to boil inside him. He told me, apropos of absolutely nothing, that what ought to be done with q——s was to take every one of them and hang them up by the b——s from the bell tower of the Cathedral. If you could have seen how my magical lion taming had him eating out of my hand last night! He spread his legs like a little lamb waiting to be sprinkled with dewdrops! When at last I stabbed him with my muscular dagger, he was on all fours, wagging his tail in happiness. He moaned and begged me to plunge it to the center of his soul."

"Have you finished telling me your gross stories? Don't you feel any shame at all, talking in such a way?"

Recounting his adventures brought no blush to his cheek at all; much less did wallowing in the enjoyment of his debauches. It did not even distress him that Abelardo might come to know of his nocturnal descents into the mud.

The wanton libertinage of Chevalier betokened the degree of confusion and incoherence to which the world had descended in our century. It was like Chaos, the fruit of Water reacting with Fire, Air with Earth.

You, though, would come into the world so that all might be ordered and have meaning. Hallelujah!

22

HOW ALIVE TO ME STILL IS THE MEMORY OF
that evening when Benjamin, at six years of age, first played
Chopin's Waltz in A-flat Major! His little hands flew effortlessly over the keyboard; and yet by the time he began
to achieve fame as a pianist, he had already unwittingly
begun the labors of Hercules. But how ignorant I was of
that then! I did not know that Music, linked to Grace, reveals
its nature, more celestial than earthly, without hindrance,
let, or moderation; nor did I know that it was the divine
breath of Music that had broken down the wall of incom-
prehension erected between our ancestors at the foot of the
Tower of Babel.

When I set Benjamin to his exercises on the piano, I
possessed no greater intellectual baggage than my own scarce
knowledge, and no greater illumination than my ignorance.

How wonderfully improved I would be when I welcomed you into the world!

That night I dreamt that a little girl tumbled from the top of a gigantic bottle, and that she fell into a bath of stars, while a wise female monkey, banging randomly on a typewriter, was composing a sonnet. Then the Sun and the Moon dived into the pool of stars with the little girl, and the natures of the three were utterly transformed.

The next night I had another dream. First I heard voices shouting, "They are murdering the innocents!" Then a very learned woman appeared, and she extracted the dew that contained the spirit of a murdered girl. The wise woman poured the extract into the pure, but inert, body of a dove, as a symbol of the resplendent child.

After your birth it was not hard for me to paint my dreams, and to interpret them as they flowed forth. Chevalier, however, was prevented by the nature of his wit, so sluggish and nonsensical, from making even the least effort to interpret them. How delighted he was, though, when I narrated them to him, some from the inside, some from the outside!

"Things are the way they are. One shouldn't go mucking about in the Not-Here, digging up sullied garlands."

Had Chevalier been an Initiate, he would have possessed only the keys that opened the arcana of the short, dry, easy Way. I, on the contrary, was always enthralled by the long, humid, thankless Way, the way taught me, from books, and with equal doses of charity and perseverance, by the Masters I took as my own.

23

THE ACCUMULATING FRUSTRATIONS AND DIS-
appointments surprised me less than they disheartened me,
but Chevalier's wit did not cool:

"If you want a procreator, as you so pedantically call him,
for your child, get out of those parlors of yours and look
for him a thousand miles from home. What do you expect
from those timid little dried-up cornhusk dolls that your
class calls 'men'? You've got to find yourself some uncouth
lowlife, some savage, some crude beast of a man, a brass-
balled lady-killer in spats, an unscrupulous rounder, a rogue.
Let yourself get mugged by some holdup man who'll lay
on with a vengeance. Open your dewy self like the petals
of a flower to some foul pirate, and you'll see how fast he'll
make you a mother, how fast he'll fill your womb with the
smell of lilies and stables, how fast he'll bestow his disre-

spectful homage upon you! You'll be galloping across the plains of pleasure with your loins unbuttoned to the wind."

Chevalier knew that his incessant flow of substanceless words, his melancholy and excrementitious babblings were of little succor but rather great distress to me.

"You are insulting my plan with that sick pornographic novel you so delight in inventing for yourself. I will face the moment of truth with not the slightest shadow of carnal pleasure."

He looked me up and down, from head to feet, with a smirk of gleeful derision, as though I had suddenly been turned into some bizarre freak.

"You'll go to the altar like chaste Joseph did with Mary!"

Chevalier could make himself a nuisance to me, as a fly might, but he could not truly offend me. I began to hear his message through his verbal fireworks: he was right, I had taken a tortuous and ill-paved route—one that I well knew might fail to lead me to the ends I sought.

"Change your tack, forget these well-mannered neighbors of yours that are incapable of going into the bullring even against a toothpick. You need a rebel with fire in his eyes, a beast that will gore you."

This modification of my plan neither improved nor besmirched the symbolic meaning of your arrival on this earth, and so I agreed to it, as though I were a driver with a learner's permit. It was true, so far I had grappled with those defaming and pusillanimous men and issued from the combat without a scratch.

How impatient I was to see you born!

2 4

TIME EATS AWAY, CORRODES, WEARS DOWN, and splinters my recollections. They lose sharpness, but the meaning remains. How the goodness and simplicity of my father shine in the mirror of memory!

At three, Benjamin was the fixed geometric center of the house. My father revolved around him as though on a treadmill of rapture. Benjamin, all unwittingly, healed my father with the childlike, ingenuous, but perfectly fitting words he spoke. With simple and innocent stubbornness he transformed him, he amputated his superfluous attachments, cutting into his living flesh.

My father stopped going to the Club at night to see his friends. His only friend now was Benjamin. He would look at him in mute wonder, abandoning every temptation of creative thought, every reflection that did not first pass through the fine sieve of admiration. Little by little he was transformed into an absolute parasite, an artificial ruin. He trembled, he bowed to the whims of his daughter's son, more than half a century younger than he. As deaf to his wife's cutting sarcasm as he was to the whispering of the servants, he happily worshiped a child, in what was probably the most loving act of his life. How my father would have loved you had he known you!

As the years passed, I could only marvel at Benjamin's unconscious ability to raise the incombustible principles of Music to their ultimate purification.

I dreamt that a huge female lizard slithered out of an oven in which pies were being baked, and that it breathed out a fire that burned a child-queen who wore three crowns; the grandest of the three represented her bastardy. The lizard swaddled her in several diapers and then put her, now become a bean, into a gigantic Epiphany cake. When the lizard asked for some sugar to sprinkle over it, a lady pianist brought a little shaker that bore the inscription "Philosophers' Salt."

25

WITH A DEGREE OF ABANDON UNWONTED
even for himself, Chevalier reveled frenziedly during Carnival, careless of the fact that his friend Abelardo, immobilized in his bed, was awaiting him at home. He would
paint his lips as well as his eyebrows and cheeks.

"It's been five weeks now since your father died. Mourning sits well only upon spinsters."

My grief had not abated; the routines it guided me into
could not so quickly lead to indifference. Neither the volume
nor the quality of the suffering had varied since my beloved
father's death. As real, as positive, as concrete as Physics was
my grief, and its consequences as tangible as Chemistry's.
External stimuli did not budge it; only logic, reason, and
experience could.

I treasured the memory of my father, in respect of his
kindness and good sense. I missed his candor and simplicity

as I would have an eye torn from my head. How fittingly, how rightly I had loved him, and he me! Between us there had never crept any sentiment that had not first been sifted by thoughtfulness and reflection.

I only learned the inestimable worth of his gestures, his remarks, his smiles, when death promoted them to the rank of invisible heirlooms. Strolling with me a few weeks before his death, he attempted to dispel the misgivings I had, by saying:

"How is it possible that two witnesses such as you and I could have been victims of the same illusion?"

My father, in spite of his sincerity, uprightness, and transparency, was suggesting to me the absurd idea that Benjamin had been only a mirage.

So many nights my beloved father would sit, trying to escape his melancholy, at the piano, in the very figure of Benjamin! He would pretend to play, though without touching the keys even with the tips of his wandering fingers, as though that might allay his longing. And with what incomparably sweet harmony did he indulge that whim of his!

26

HOW MANY TIMES, IN MY DREAMS, DURING
that Carnival and its discordant and chaotic revelry, did I
see you as you would be!

One night I dreamt that four winged animals stood motionless in the sky. You were there, under them, halfway
up the sky, sitting on two "wheels of fire." You stood watch,
while the two wheels revolved without burning you. I realized, suddenly, that you were spinning with a distaff,
though keeping the flame always alive.

Wishing to play the part of matchmaker so that—at
last!—the preface to your conception might be written,
Chevalier racked his brain for candidates.

"Last night, during the ritual of the burial of the sardine,
I found your man. He's a little stud pony, blind and legless,
but he's got good aim."

Even when he was speaking about my plan, Chevalier let himself be carried away by vulgarity and uncouthness, and by other, still worse ravings and bizarre notions as well, rather than speaking with scientific respect.

"You've got to write S—— a letter that will inspire him to f—— you. You've got to let him know that you're waiting for him like a cat in heat, all alone, impatient, and purring with lust. You'll see, he'll jump at you without a parachute. He's a skeleton pickled in torrents of hot lather. He dreams of thrusting himself into your womb and kicking like a grasshopper."

I wrote this man a letter as measured as it was precise. As I told him, I unfortunately had to wait five days, so that the plan might be undertaken at the perfect moment—the moment determined, with strict exactitude, by my menstrual flow.

How I would have liked my body to be dotted with openings of transparent crystal so that I might observe the stages of your evolution within my womb!

From the moment I discovered that, against all the frowns of Fortune, I was about to take the first step toward the realization of my project, how I redoubled my care and foresight! Yet in empirical terms I knew that I could not foresee all the details and circumstances of the crucial event.

How I loved you already!

27

WITH THAT COOL RELIEF, I SPENT THE FIVE
days that preceded your conception consulting books, ex-
amining old engravings, and meditating intensively. Although at that time I was learned in the gestures and postures
of carnal pleasure and in the occult meaning that they veiled,
I discovered unsuspected tones and shades which I carefully
analyzed. I perceived that there was a certain analogy between the act I was to consummate with the procreator and
the fact of your birth per se. A subtle kinship linked them.
They presented themselves to my thought as two distinct,
and even physically antagonistic, phases, though of one same
nature and even of the same substance. How blessed waiting
for you made me feel!

I dreamt of you every night, without exception.

In one of those dreams, a frenzied rooster, with the image
of an oak tattooed on its crest, was transformed into a Phoe-

nix as it gave one of its exultant leaps. I fed it ashes mixed with sand. Then you washed your hands with water that did not wet them, because it was dry. At that moment, a silent fox arrived, impenetrable and hermetic. Gazing at you fixedly, it dropped, delicately, a few drops of Mercury into a crystal mortar, and when they coagulated they became Sulfur.

I glossed these signs with the light of clear truth, and therefore I wondered whether I should not conceive you with my head down and my feet above, as though I were crucified. I soon discarded the idea because, in spite of its advantages, it might be uncomfortable for your progenitor.

The profound meaning of the act, only I could grasp. How naive it would have been to expect him to understand it! He would not even be able to comprehend its philosophical, social, and moral properties. My energy and my invincibility would allow me to maintain control during the episode. This vigilance would be my greatest guarantee against any rupture.

I tempered my wide-flung impatience with the balm of foresightedness. Once born, you would live in a universe so different from that of other people! So many of them, employing the language of parable, thought they could communicate to me truths insidiously adulterated with falsifications, half-truths that might misguide me in the end. I, however, would never confuse you! I swore that on the most sacred.

2 8

TO THE THROBBING OF MY OWN EXPECTANCY
Chevalier and Abelardo also lived the last few days—Chevalier, beside himself with excitement tinged with monomania, and Abelardo, his curiosity restrained by prudence and good sense.

Because of his illness, Abelardo lived in exile from the world of his friend, but Chevalier did communicate his opinions to me. The two men dwelt together in a two-story house which overlooked the estuary. When Abelardo's daily rest-cure periods ended, he restored old paintings, miniatures especially. He never went out.

"The poor creature is exhausted. His consumption weakens his lungs and grinds down his strength. It is like tooth decay in the soul. Since he can no longer make the effort to go up and down the stairs, he doesn't even go into the garden anymore. His breathing is faint and labored."

The root, branch, and stem of Abelardo's conversation, wrapped in exquisite garments, was, Chevalier reported, my motherhood. But the plan had been conceived in me, it needed me for its realization, and it could take form only in my body. In spite of the necessary profane and outward intervention of the procreator, it obeyed the exact functioning of my own natural laws. And yet Abelardo clung to the illusion that he would be present on the night of my fertilization.

It took me some time to realize that the absence of light appears as an essential requisite for all fecundation. Nature conceives in utter darkness; mushrooms, for example, are born, couple, and grow during the night. It was thanks to my nightly rest that my own organism regathered its strength, that my cells, worn away and stolen by the light of day, were renewed.

Making the decision to conceive you at night was the prologue to the book of my destiny.

29

CHEVALIER WAS SO BESIDE HIMSELF WITH trivialities that he got it into his head to imagine you dressed in blue:

"It is the symbolic color of the evening star."

How he wanted to credit the notion that he would be a participant in the act, in which I was to be but a mere intermediary. How blinded he was by impatience! He was mad to see with his own eyes and apprehend with his own senses the instant of my fecundation:

"As a traveler, or as a pilgrim, since I will not be able to sign on as pilot, nor even as supernumerary deckhand."

The night that preceded my appointment with the progenitor, Chevalier had a dream that terrified him. He could make out a series of hallucinations, each one linked to the next—an eagle struggling with a dragon, a warrior squashing a serpent at the foot of an oak tree, a giant cutting off a hydra's heads, a scarlet viper strangling a green scorpion in its coils, a horse trampling a salamander, and a little girl shooting a raging tiger with an arrow.

More than by the subject of his dream, my attention was held by the disturbance of his senses as he recounted it to me. His pessimistic interpretation fit the circumstances admirably, but it suffered from improbability, and it wounded my conscience and my sense of proportion.

I was unable to test Chevalier's certainty by the operations of reason; the violence of his manner affected me not in the least, neither in its conclusions nor in its elements; much less was I affected by the crude obscenity that so tormented him. No base or lewd sentiment ever cast its shadow on the essence of my plan.

The last few hours brought me introspection and serenity. I withstood both internal pressures and comforts, so that Nature might act with integrity. I restrained myself, with the greatest quietude, and grew mute and docile. Reflecting on the grace I was about to receive with such unfathomable simplicity, I withdrew into myself and meditated.

You would arrive, now, as the most precious gift of Nature.

30

AFTER I HAD READ THE FIRST VOLUME OF
the work, in my beloved father's library, I could at last affirm
that "I am that I am." From that moment onward, more
sensible than ever before to the bright clear lights of truth,
I placed body and soul at the service of the workings of the
progenitor's seed.

Three hours before the man was to penetrate the sanctum
of my room, and of my body, I began to ready myself,
without hurry but without pause. I bathed myself thor-
oughly; I set my feet in a basin and sprinkled them with
water from the washbasin, thinking of you constantly.

Weaving a web of compliments about me, Chevalier did
not stir from my room until the final moment. He exhibited
signs of both nervousness and timidity.

The night before the procreation I dreamt that you were
sitting at my side on the bank of a river, and that you were

baiting fish hooks. You disguised them within a rubbery paste. Beside us there was a geometer fishing; on his pole he caught a porcelain fish, which was actually the Sun— but how tiny it was! We raised our heads and saw, in the center of Ursa Major, like some auspicious omen, the Pole Star.

How Abelardo wanted to go as Chevalier's second during those last hours of waiting in my house! But his illness held him prisoner, the sheets of his bed his bonds. Chevalier set up a little table for him, its legs cut down so that he could restore his paintings while still bound to his bed. A short while before he left me alone with my resolve, Chevalier spoke to me words filled with emotion and sincerity:

"I shall never deceive Abelardo again. This time it's not just some vain promise; I will keep it, I swear. I swear by all I hold dearest, now that you yourself are wavering between the abyss and the most profound vertigo."

Still unpossessed by calm, Chevalier took his leave of me. I wrapped myself in a white sheet and awaited the pro-creator.

How wise the book of Nature is to hoard within its pages the keys to the arcana and to Science!

I thought of you, and could not keep myself from feelings of euphoria.

31

WHEN THE PROCREATOR STOOD ON THE
threshold of my room proffering obscenities, I listened, ready
to carry out my mission, to his first phrases. His words did
not surprise me, nor did the tone of slight sarcasm in which
they were cloaked. For a few minutes I had to adopt as my
own the dress, the language, and the customs of that brazen
lecher wallowing in his base ways.

"Here I am, at your service, madam."

I knew that everything that was about to occur lay in
the realm of the attainable. By a slow, methodical process I
had readied my spirit. My senses lay numb and somnolent,
remote from the eventual, and aleatory, disturbances that
impended.

Before embarking on the act per se, he whispered to me
jumbled, impetuous words, speaking nonsense about his desires and his depraved appetites.

"You are naked under that sheet, w——! You f——
turn me on!"

I had foreseen everything, save that he might speak to
me. But if my person satisfied his tastes and his appetites,
as in the grossest way he seemed to be indicating it did, I
could not understand why he insisted on drawing out the
wait by telling me so in such dilatory terms. How I would
have preferred that without a word, without a glance, without a touch, he go straight to the act! It was not easy to see
the connection between his gestures and his contradictory
words. I feared that this behavior might become at last
an obstacle to the path I had laid out. He went on, insis-
tently pouring out his wild and extravagant fantasies to
me, fantasies filthy with adulation, lies, and hypocritical
unctuousness.

"What a f—— idea! Going to bed the first time we've
ever seen each other, like *that*! It would have made me even
hotter if you'd been waiting for me in bed with your eyes
blindfolded."

Following my plan, I turned off the light, and I lay back
onto the bed. I feared that his intellectual disorder and his
depravity would lead to no positive or scientific good. Yet
at the same time I was filled with enormous hopefulness. I
knew that I would isolate the pure component of his mass
when I received the Sign and the first manifestation of the
operation. Nature and this act, in perfect balance, would
bring about your conception. Mistress of my own will, absolute monarch of my own wisdom and learning, I set the
whole of my wit to meditating upon the ways of access to
serenity before the imminence of that memorable event.

32

ALTHOUGH WE ARE ALL SURROUNDED BY THE same flesh, during the first part of the operation I seemed to myself so different from the models I had seen in books. I felt imprisoned, like a dove whose feet had been bound to two stones.

I was assaulted by the irrational fear that my womb would not retain the semen, or that the drops of it would evaporate, or that they would simply vanish, or that they would be spilled without leaving me the minimum remainder necessary for their working.

I lay pensive, silent, and awestricken all at once before that marvelous, extraordinary paradigm of creation, the irrefutable model for an occult science whose secrets one day you would entirely possess.

While the coupling was being effected, the man, with as much ferocity as perseverance, was emitting incomprehensible guttural moans and cries, but through them I thought I could already hear your crystalline voice.

At no moment during the operation did I experience any vision or hallucination. I was nonetheless victim, afterward, of a nightmare; I dreamt I had been reincarnated as a cow with its legs spread open wide.

By an effort of will I completely recovered my clear-sightedness. How straight I had penetrated the mystery of creation! That alone raised me into the realm of wisdom, and heaped stores of virtue and discipline upon me.

To be worthy of your destiny, I attempted to carry sincerity and modesty to the highest peak of perfection, choking off all rashness and impetuosity and setting myself under the virtuous and diverting tutelage of serenity.

How right and just it was that nine months after that night you should emerge from the darkness, to shine like the Morning Star!

Like some extraordinary augury, the first sentence I had read in that first volume of the work declared:

"It is written that Life dwells in a space unique to it."

3 3

WHEN, FALLEN FROM HIS HEIGHTS OF
frenzy, the man concluded his jostling about, he said:

"I came!"

How infinitely joyous I felt! But routines take hold so
obstinately, and the stiff crusts of prejudice clutch so tenaciously, that the progenitor was unable to grasp the import
of the act just concluded. His discernment was clouded by
the uncivil, uncouth passion of it.

"You loved it! You were like a bitch in heat! That was
one great f——!"

Though I shunned immoderate enthusiasm, which might
have blinded my reason, I was swept away by happiness.

My plan demanded exactitude and perspicacity in the
observation of many variables. I logically, carefully, and
without undue zeal weighed what had occurred, keeping
my heart good, fervent, and pure.

For the procreator I felt a deep gratitude, but gratitude dependent solely upon my understanding.

"I can never lie, and at this moment even less so. I have experienced not the slightest libidinous satisfaction. But you, sir, have, to a certain point, brought me pleasure that you cannot imagine. I give you my heartfelt thanks for your help so that my plan can take root."

My absolute indifference to his hypotheses and his ardors disconcerted him greatly.

"That's it?"

I thought with my brain, unlike him, who was in so many different ways unschooled and uninitiate—his faculties of observation and reflection had long been blunted by lust.

"Aren't we going to see each other again?"

He pressed his attentions upon me. Smitten with desire, he offered to be my lover.

He had, like the indispensable drone he was, admirably done the work of Nature, the common Mother of us all. When the mounting was done, however, our association was dissolved forever; the progenitor now served only as a nuisance or a distracting noise.

I knew that I was the anonymous, mute disciple of Eternal Goodness.

What an extraordinarily fertile night!

34

TOO LATE I LEARNED WHAT ROOTS YOUR
trunk, your branches, and your fruits possessed! Who would
have dared foresee that seventeen years after a beginning so
wonderfully wise and promising, you, of your own volition,
would truncate your own future? What a sad and grievous
straying there was! What terrible weights of absurdity and
tedium fell upon me with the last gasp of your revolt!

Benjamin came into this world furtively, in the house of
a hole-and-corner midwife. My father painted those first
years of Benjamin's life to me in somber hues, and I knew
they had been seasoned by whispered rumors, the consequences of Lulú's flight.

Your childhood would not be blackened by such smut
and sullying. You would be born and grow up wrapped
always in the white blanket of love and serenity. You would
be surrounded by persons happy to be living with you, in

the bosom of a flowering, humane family organized scientifically. You would, I was certain, never know of poverty, or prison, or slavery. How dared you defy your fate?

"Let me touch your belly, I want to feel her when she kicks. You'll see, she'll be a ballerina. Don't get angry, woman. It's such a pretty thought—a butterfly fluttering inside a little lace tutu. Oh, come, don't be so serious, or so stuffy, either. Going around in circles all day long with that philosophy and those solemnities of yours . . ."

Before your birth, Chevalier had already adopted you. He spent praises like a king on the banquet of his admiration for you. Sometimes I thought he was almost as happy as I myself, pacing the floor, awaiting your coming. His expansiveness throbbed under his noble generosity.

Without being privy to my confidences, neither Chevalier nor Abelardo could know the purpose of my plan, for they were ignorant of the deeper motives for your being brought into the world. And when I was with them, I clung to the vow of silence I had imposed upon myself. The plan required both patience and constancy, both will and discretion, both daring and decisiveness. I never feared my own audacity, for I always prided myself on my circumspection. On the path of kindness, I discharged my inescapable duty to maintain silence.

In what marvelous state of mind I was approaching the eternity of your glory!

35

I MADE THE DECISION TO MOVE TO THE CAPI-
tal of the nation, to flee the city beclouded for me by
the scandals of Lulú and so to destroy that past once and
for all.

The decision was made, also, with an eye to ensuring
that your scrupulous upbringing would lack for nothing;
from the moment of your birth onward, you would live a
methodical life, both scientific and hygienic.

"Do you want that ballerina of yours to run hurdles like
a racehorse?"

Seconding my foresighted decision, and allowing their
affection for me to enter into their own caprice, Chevalier
and Abelardo also decided to move to the capital to live.

"Everyone is so old-fashioned here! They say such dreadful things about us! They smell like disinfectant."

As soon as I had been paid my beloved father's legacy,

my animosity stretched to the breaking, I began to pack. I stuffed the books from the library into several steamer trunks. Toward the beginning of summer, I took an express train that stopped only at the major stations. How filled with hope I was as I traveled with you nestled inside me!

I arrived alone at the North Terminal. Chevalier and Abelardo were to come three weeks later. The city at that time already harbored more than half a million inhabitants; the enormous size of that metropolis suited perfectly my desire to hide myself. After a brief stay in the Ritz, I bought a modest country house—our home!—far from the noise and bustle of the city, serene and filled with air and light. I selected the place for its garden—so healthful!—and its elevation—so salutary for the lungs! Here you would grow and develop freely, with peace, stability, and security, and enwrapped in the serenity needed for you to grow, flower, and bear fruit.

With what profound faith, what fervent confidence, what temerity, and what modesty did I undertake this phase of the plan.

During the journey on the train, as I was lulled by the rocking of the car, and all alone with my thoughts, I pictured you as a supernatural flame.

36

AS I AWAITED YOUR BIRTH, I READ AND meditated constantly, thereby freeing myself from the captivity of my anxiety and reaching the harbor of certainty. Yielding impartially to my every inclination, I let my enthusiasm lead me along all the paths of scientific, philosophical, and hygienic activity. In order to put to rout certain physical debilities, I took walks among the pines for an hour every day.

Abelardo traveled by ambulance, accompanied by Chevalier and a male nurse. They rented the cottage that bordered our estate, a residence consisting of two floors and a garden. Abelardo took, once again, a room on the second floor, but he was so ill that he could not even go down into the garden on sunny afternoons. How sad it was to see his brusque fits of irritation and to hear the foul rage with which he cursed his abominable fortune!

Chevalier showed me the tiny paintings that Abelardo, with so much skill and excellence, restored. With what astonishing mastery did Abelardo paint the chipped or missing details of the antique miniatures! It was as though imitation, and even falsification, might fill in the blanks, the chronological voids, of History and Art. I poured such praise over those small things!

Chevalier brought me the messages that Abelardo wrote on small slips of paper in a full, round hand and sent to me:

"My birth was, for my parents, a catch of the most frivolous sort. They remembered it always as an event which belonged to the realm of fable. You, however, are performing a deed so very different! How expectantly I am following its course!"

Tuberculosis had enchained Abelardo, from the age of twelve, to doctors, tests and examinations, and nurses. His illness besieged his breathing, launching attacks of coughing, asphyxiation, and bloody sputum, and showing no respect for the many medications prescribed by whim and almost at random. His family suffocated him so, that he emerged from his childhood in exhaustion, and with no improvement to his lungs to show for it. You, on the contrary, would live your life within a community crowned by the most dazzling jewels of civilization.

How happily, how pleasantly I spent my while, predicting and chronicling the events of your life to come!

37

HOW QUICKLY CHEVALIER FORGOT HIS PROM-
ises of faithfulness! How many nights did he go out, leaving
Abelardo alone in his solitary room! He would return
toward dawn, as exhausted and downcast as he had been
euphoric and overexcited when he left. His disease, I believed, stemmed more from his humors than from his organs.

"What can I do, my dear, for your ballerina? Unless you
intend to dedicate her to the magical arts of illusion and
prestidigitation."

How terribly it grieved me that he should call you a
"ballerina."

Chevalier, shunning poverty, sinned by excess. The
plethora of his emotions as well might come out in unbridled
jubilation as in tortured bouts of anguish. On occasion, his
conscience tormented him:

"I am a worse leech upon him than his tuberculosis bugs. I live at his expense, I feed upon the fruit of his labors, I sleep in the house that he pays for, and I take advantage of his weakness to deceive him. How his silence howls in the darkness of my remorse!"

Abelardo never reproached his friend, nor did Chevalier's nocturnal outings draw from him the slightest comment. He never, in even the most imperceptible way, slighted Chevalier.

"As though he didn't see what was going on! He eats sawdust and ashes in the privacy of his solitude."

Chevalier alternated between liveliness and pathos, but his seriousness was always spangled with his sparks and sputters of wit. He would wrestle with language, curvetting and caracoling with circumlocution, in an attempt to point up the delicacy of his intelligence, the sorrows of his soul, and the transports of his desperate passion. But my obligation was to you; I strove to understand everything, explain everything. How clear-sightedly I reasoned, aided by truth and impartiality!

My soul soothed by an extraordinary balm, by insistent and delicious thoughts, I could feel you growing large inside my womb. I reflected that from the day of your birth onward you would captivate hearts without offending spirits. How joyously and profitably I believed in you! How I loved you already!

38

DURING THE NINE MONTHS OF MY PREG-
nancy, in conversation only with myself, how much I dreamt
of you! One night, in my dreams, I saw you standing under
an arcade; with your finger you were pointing out to me,
in a large volume lying open on a table, a maxim that I
could not make out. In spite of the peace that reigned all
about, I caught a glimpse, in a mirror, of a vigorous, athletic
woman strangling a hyena, while two other young women
motionlessly embraced one another, paying no attention to
that sacrifice. Suddenly a flash of lightning illuminated the
arcade, and I could read the maxim: "Science governs Love
and Energy."

I was convinced that you would repudiate the chaos of
the civilizations now in fashion, which had barely risen above
barbarity, and that you would achieve the fusion of a vast
spirit with a logical intelligence. In that enterprise, I would

assist you as a most humble servant. How bright and smiling the days would dawn!

"My daughter will not have a childhood."

Chevalier was scandalized by my determination, holding it up as an exemplar of hubris and preciosity.

"What you want to do is make one of those affected bluestockings out of her, a woman as haughty and fatuous as yourself. Stop all this pontification. You can't turn your daughter's childhood into a wake, with no yo-yos. You've got to play with dirt and with flowers, with kites that snap their strings and lizards with cigarette butts dangling from the corners of their mouths."

A short while before your birth, I saw, from a distance, and for the first time, Abelardo sitting on a stone bench in the garden of his cottage. With his bald head fringed with white hair, he looked much older than Chevalier. There was an air of such peace about him, as though his express mission consisted in translating the truths that Chevalier, deaf to the calls of integrity, unwittingly gathered.

"I saw Abelardo from the balcony of my room."

"He thinks he might infect your daughter and you. That's why he doesn't want to come into physical contact with you. One must respect a sick man's whims."

39

"ALLOW ME TO GO ON DENYING MYSELF YOUR presence. It will be best for your daughter, in her day."

Accompanying that message, which gave some relief to my desire to see him, Abelardo sent me a drawing in pastels. It was a landscape with a volcano in eruption and a snow-capped mountain peak. A stream crossed the valley from right to left. The center of the composition was dominated by a gigantic crystal flask, from which emerged three huge flower buds that resembled pomegranates. At the neck of the crystal vessel, there was a child floating in the water; inside the globe of the vessel, a man and a woman, almost nude, wearing crowns and intertwining their fingers, gazed out at the viewer enigmatically.

A few months before you were born, Chevalier disappeared for two days. Abelardo took up vigil at the garden gate, patiently awaiting his return. But how filled with fears and torments his spirit was! On one occasion he turned his head toward the balcony where I was sitting in a wicker chair, observing him. How imperturbable his expression seemed as he smiled at me!

I recalled my beloved father. How many nights had he too awaited the impossible return of Benjamin, and with what apparent impassivity! My father contemplated the eclipse of his life with such listlessness. He slipped, regardlessly, from disappointment into death. His hopelessness distilled a secret, sour ferment in his soul. When night fell, his humble, withdrawn demeanor would reveal the desolation that rose like dark smoke from the deepest depths of his grief. For hours he would sit and gaze at the piano scores that had awakened Benjamin's genius.

My father believed himself a failure: his daughter had chosen a vile and dishonored path, he had been unable to pull out the rebellious roots that clutched at his wife's loins, and Benjamin had vanished, like a mirage, at the moment of his greatest love for him.

Having lost all confidence in human sympathy, he feared that those fierce disillusionments would prevent me from looking, with love and affection, within him and perceiving his soul.

40

ONE MORNING, JUST AT DAWN, I WAS AWAK-
ened by bitter, angry shouting, without any apparent cause.
I recognized to my great sorrow the voice of Chevalier. He
was engaged in a heated argument, so far as I could tell,
with a young man, about his own age, in the street, at the
garden gate of the cottage.

Abelardo, wrapped in a shawl, staggered back from the
gate, his spirit assailed by spoiled and rotten dreams. He
had been sitting up, waiting for Chevalier all night in
the garden, but he did not want to pry into the crowd of
mysteries that peopled his friend's nights. Thus, he ran toward his house, fleeing as quickly as his ebbing strength
allowed him.

With what vulgarities the young man insulted Chevalier!
But Chevalier replied in kind. Paradoxically, their traded
obscenities emitted, in spite of their fury, a smell of must

and mildew, an odor of the grave, the dry fragrance of withered flowers. The two men abused each other like the two original creatures of a vanished humanity, of a forgotten world. Chevalier wept when the two at last foundered and sank into a long silence freighted with hate.

Abelardo watched the row for a moment through the blinds in his room. With melancholy seeping drop by drop into him, into his very bones, he stepped back. The vision of that quarrel, that vulgar squabble, oppressed him like a nightmare.

The young man's fist smashed viciously into Chevalier's face; then he cursed him, and at last he spat on him. His nose gushing blood, Chevalier staggered to the cottage and opened the door, though with intentional cunning he sought refuge in the garden. In spite of the distance between us, I caught a foul acid smell that stopped my throat.

How I grieved as I tumbled into my bed! I felt you lying within the wet vault of my womb, protected, as you would always be, by my lucidity and my goodness.

41

HIS PERVERSE RECREATIONS AND HIS twisted inclinations had brought Chevalier face-to-face with the contortions of fury. After the fight, he slept for eighteen hours. Abelardo cared for his bruises lovingly, putting his compassion before the hurt and jealousy he felt.

So as to secure the most favorable conditions for your delivery, I made contact with a famous obstetrician. Medicine, combined with Experience, would stand beside me during my labor—although the finest specialist was incapable of penetrating the dynamic mystery that would preside over your entry into the world.

I queried Nature day and night in order to understand under what conditions, under the sway of what will, that unexampled creation would be brought to pass. In the laboratory of my womb so many elements were being compounded . . . I believed I had discovered the occult energies under whose influences the gestation was taking place. With such keen delight I felt you coming!

The obstetrician only reticently accepted my case. He was unable to accept the fact that his science was patently incapable of formulating a logical, accurate explanation of birth.

"Please don't worry. Believe me, I can tell you without exaggeration that you are in the best of hands. No one understands Obstetrics better than I. Put all those queer ideas out of your head. Of course I don't find them strange, nor do they surprise me. In fact, they're part of what's taught under the rubric *Fancies in the Pregnant Patient*."

Veiling my skepticism with modesty, I resolved to keep a watch on him, for I knew that he, Professor of Medicine that he was, could only credit the certainties and arrogant conceits of his own ambitious brain. Constant empiricism had little by little deluded him, for empiricism is an old madness, and an incurable mania.

Your material embodiment and your spiritual essence could not be dissociated simply by the fiat of the reigning positivism of the age.

Light is but rarefied and spiritualized Fire. And you would be so radiant!

42

WHEN I BEGAN TO TEST HIS FIDELITY, MAK-
ing adroit soundings of his conscience, Chevalier promised,
once again, to stop going out at night.

"I swear by all that's sacred that I will never again deceive
Abelardo."

As he declared with great firmness that he could not be
faulted with any sin more grave than that of being a victim,
he showed me his body covered with scars like trails of
solder.

"Look what that whore has done to me! I was brought
into this world to do nothing but suffer! I'm more alone
than absence itself, more abandoned than oblivion itself,
more nauseating than putrescent filth. Comfort me!"

The dejected Chevalier brought darkness to his own
world, like a black sun become a cold and lifeless star. But
what a short time his spells of disillusionment lasted!

"I'm sorry for Abelardo especially. He hasn't said a word to me, but I can imagine what he's thinking. He is so weak, so frail! I'm sure he's afraid that if he complains I'll get angry and leave him. I disgust myself. I'm nothing but a sponger and a leech. A sickening parasite."

Abelardo sent me a message written on a little porcelain cup with a mohair brush:

"I've heard that you have some doubt about the obstetrician. I am convinced that he will not fail you during your labor. No one can spoil what Nature has confected. Allow me to congratulate you for your unwavering perseverance."

How seldom do men of science, like the obstetrician, possess a truly scientific spirit! How wrinkled and gray they are, and how cursedly infected with gross rationalism!

That night I dreamt that you were leading me by the hand down a street lined with cabarets. A cast-iron lioness came up to us, gave a strange leap, and at last took a heraldic pose. A tiny woman dressed as a page offered us a tiny barrel transfixed by an arrow.

43

ONE WEEK BEFORE YOUR BIRTH I DREAMT
that you talked like a bird. You were standing atop a tower,
dressed in the robes of a Philosopher-Virgin, and you bore
a torch in your hand. A chair and a harquebus were bal-
anced, swaying, on a tightrope. On the terrace, a female
doctor in a top hat was polishing pieces of gold which she
then stacked, one by one, at the foot of the tower. When
she finished, the harquebus went off and golden sparkles
shot forth from your torch.

I was convinced that you would speak a phonetic language based solely on assonance, the language of the birds.
You would perceive the spirit of everything written or spoken, more than its literal meaning.

Chevalier, his brain sprawling and indolent, twisted my
interpretation of the dream into a thing as superficial as it
was sentimental.

"We will hear, from the bank of the stream, the warbling of your ballerina flying along with the foam."

Another night I dreamt that a tiny little man, as naked as the day he was born, was sitting on Nature's Stone of Wisdom explaining to you the original language from which all other tongues derived—the language used by Adam when he gave names to all the things of creation, the language of the birds, a language that is instinct, and that is the voice of Nature.

"If you keep telling me dreams like that one, I'm going to be forced to tell you that you're a scatterbrained know-it-all."

Even when I explained my most sensible ideas to him, Chevalier would become the shameless buffoon and laugh. But when I saw the watercolor that Abelardo had painted for me, I realized that Chevalier had told his friend my dreams. In this painting there figured three Incas, all identical, bearing three different inscriptions: "Diplomatic Language," "Courtly Language," and "Universal Language."

That night, overwhelmed by nostalgia, I played the piano, like Benjamin, and the music lifted me, dizzyingly, to the highest pinnacles of truth.

44

CHEVALIER'S WIT WAS SUFFICIENT UNTO ALL
the surprises that followed from his lecherous and intemperate life. Yet when he declared that he couldn't "see"
something, it was because he unconsciously felt that he could
invariably "see" Nature.

"You think that this original language your daughter
will use is already understood by animals. What madness!
I swear to you that my speech is the precise mold of my
thought."

That is why he so often expressed himself as though he
preferred painstakingly ornamented falsehood to the naked
truth. He took enormous delight in veiled fawning and
flattering preciosities.

As the date of your birth drew day by day nearer, Chevalier's fantasies grew ever more outlandish. He pictured you breakfasting on gruel and hot chocolate, playing with puppets and Punch and Judy dolls, and dancing in a gauze tutu.

"I too will be, like you, something of a mother to her."

How Abelardo would have wished to be at my side during your delivery! Chevalier, to please him, had promised to tell him every detail of my impressions, my emotions, and even my pains.

The two last visits I paid the obstetrician, who was withdrawn into the arrogance produced by his convictions, into the vanity of pride and conceit, disappointed me. For him your birth was just one more birth.

"Have confidence in Medicine. You, my dear, are too young for such wise and brainy thoughts. You're tiring yourself."

He was mistaken, for thanks to the control and the methodical system that I had imposed on myself, I remained always in a state of perfect rest and repose, not to mention that I followed a strict regimen of healthful food and hygienic walks.

"I'm talking about *mental* exhaustion. Stop indulging in all these metaphysical lucubrations. Giving birth is the most natural act in a normal woman's life."

As a faithful adherent to the cult of infallible Medicine, the obstetrician, untroubled by the fatigue of exercising his brain, did not discuss things, he pronounced. Books, which set vanity in print and which he had studied in the School of Medicine, had taught him to take appearances for reality.

Goodness, study, and serenity alone led me toward you.

4 5

I WAS IN THE GARDEN WHEN I THREW OFF the girdle of my impatience and clutched at my hopes, feeling the first pains. Night had just fallen, and Chevalier, violating his word—a vice inherent to profligacy—had gone out, dressed in a tuxedo.

Those first pains announced the commencement of labor, but even as they wrapped me in a fog of suffering, they offered me such luminous happiness!

Abelardo had observed his friend's surreptitious escape. He spent the night of your birth waiting for Chevalier, behind the garden wall, playing host to his horrible imaginings.

Chevalier had seemed to me, a few days earlier, to be so irritated by the expectancy that my pregnancy aroused in Abelardo!

"He is acting as though he were your husband. He is captured and enraptured within the magic circle of the shadow of your belly, surrounded by swelling and ever growing fears and trembling hopes."

The pains increased inexorably. Therefore, with all my energies I quickened my intelligence, sharpened my memory, and intensified my will. If my conscious self remained constantly alert, the labor would act itself out under its good auspices.

I had to wait two hours for the obstetrician's arrival, sometimes complaining and other times with moderation and temperateness.

I had a first hallucination brought on by my worsening distress. I saw a royal palace through which women philosophers strolled, carrying scalpels and forceps. I had been taken into the throne room, and my belly had become a red-hot furnace. The philosopher-women were picking up burning coals with their forceps and laying them on my loins. Before your birth, how I feared I would not be able to bear the burning of my belly!

That same nightmare, with pardonable exceptions, followed by a long-drawn-out bout of visions, gnawed at me until the moment of your birth.

At the most terrible moment of my suffering, when the pains seemed almost to be wrestling one with another, I was struck by the certainty that you were your own Seed.

46

WHAT PAIN I HAD TO SUFFER SO THAT YOU might be born! I found all the doors both of impassibility and of unconsciousness closed to me. The pain made of the bed a burning oven and of the sheets fiery coals.

Feeling as though I had been plunged into a vat of boiling tar, I saw the obstetrician arrive. A woman accompanied him.

"This is the midwife."

I could not bear the fact that a woman such as that, a quack with no scientific education, should touch my belly.

"Be still! The midwife is going to help me. Don't get upset."

An obstetrician of his reputation aided by a gypsy! What excuses he made for his outrageous ideas!

"No, I will not throw out the midwife. How can you

ask me to do such a thing! She's here for your own good. I know Science, and she knows Life."

That secret fraternity between Medicine and Hocus-Pocus horrified me. In order to protect you, however, I spoke no anathema against her. Patience is the stairway that philosophers must scale, and humility, the gate that leads into their garden.

I saw, in a flash as though from a dream, those philosopher-women with their forceps standing around the furnace of my loins, crying "Giddy-up, giddy-up!" A gigantic horse appeared, flying through the air, its front hoofs enveloped in a black cloud. Then other horses, stabbed and dying, glided by belly up, some with their legs cut off. Glowing, red-hot coals dripped from their wounds onto my belly.

"You're delirious! You'll suffer too much if you're not sedated. I'm going to show you how you ought to go through labor."

From a distance I could see myself drugged by a pain that grew more and more intense. I felt like bellowing. How alone I was, how abandoned! I was in the hands of that midwife, whose presence was an insult to all of science. I lost consciousness of everything but the suffering, which increased at every moment, and one would almost have said that the obstetrician's efforts were aimed more at maintaining the pain than at removing it. And yet, how your essence already consoled me! I would not allow myself to be dragged into the chaos of the imprudent.

47

AS I JOURNEYED THROUGH EVERY STEP AND
station of that awful agony, I could not even burst out in
sobs. Everything that had to be suffered so that you might
be born, I knew about. How many books had I not read!
I was ready, and I was resolved. You called out to me with
such spirit!

The midwife, palpating my state with her eyes, shouted
orders to me confusedly and unsystematically:

"Open your knees wider! Put your head back! Push!
Squeeze! Heave up, pretend there's a lever under you!"

Within my womb there burned like Sulfur in combustion
that primal substance that bathed you and enwrapped you.
The nightmares came fast, one after another, their common
thread the vision of my loins transformed into a boiling
caldron. In one of those nightmares, I saw an enormous
female dog with several menacing heads coming toward me,

and I knew she was going to devour and burn me. In another, my father was going into an ancient castle in flames, where he was going to be burned alive. Meanwhile, Benjamin and Lulú were competing in a musical contest with burning instruments. Benjamin perished on a pyre of pianos.

How difficult it was, in the midst of such torment and intense pain, to keep my clear-sightedness intact. You were coming to me, I could see you, you were crossing the threshold into life. But I could also hear your voice and listen to your speech.

A few seconds before your birth I had my last hallucination. A lion and a lioness were looking fixedly at each other. Each of them had a brightly glowing human mask, like a sun, lying between its paws.

The pain clouded my brain, but did not darken my lucidity. That vision of the two lions suggested to me that you would be endowed with both masculine principle and feminine virtue, that you would inherit a nature both positive and negative, and that there would be created thereby a compound substance more or less sapient, in and of itself.

You now began to emerge at the threshold of the gate of my loins, and you looked out at the universe as the Mirror of Nature.

48

I LAY PANTING, EXHAUSTED, AND SUPINE. How near seemed the arms of despair! Pain and effort had drained me utterly, when at last I heard your cry! Mingled light and shadow announced that you were now the face and aspect of the world.

"It's a *wonderful* girl! And how *roly-poly* she is!"

Suffering evaporated, leaving no dregs but relief. What great joy and peace attended that state of grace to which your birth had given rise! Nature had worked within her sphere, alone and within herself, shaping and perfecting herself so that you might be the fruit of that gestation. When you were born, spattered with blood and sprinkled with the liquid of the womb, you already possessed grace, by the act of that double baptism.

The midwife washed you. Suddenly, I ceased to see her as an obstacle in my way. The obstetrician three times styled you "wonderful" and "roly-poly," without troubling my calm after the tempest or tarnishing my golden fortune. How easy it was for me to forgive that absurdity into which his folly plunged him to the hilt!

How your little body reddened and took life as it was warmed by the bright fire that you already bore within you. As I watched you, I could feel my burning pain gradually turn into incarnate word. What jubilee, as unknown to me as it was intense, overwhelmed my senses!

With goodness as guide, and within the feeble means I had, the narrow space of my body, the most wondrous operations of the universe had been carried out! From such insignificant cause, such incommensurable effect!

How sorry I was that my father could not be with us then, when his life was being carried and passed on, when his roots had put forth new green shoots.

Abelardo sent me a message of congratulation:

"I followed the delivery from my garden. I am almost as happy as you. I know that your virtues will stand your daughter in good stead. I now understand, thanks to you, that to create is to wrest All from the Nothing of the void."

Underneath the message he had sketched the Garden of the Hesperides, at whose center stood the Tree of Life, and inside its trunk, enclosed in a transparent hollow, a little girl.

49

AS SOON AS THE OBSTETRICIAN AND THE MID-
wife left the room in which you had been born, Chevalier
appeared, crying, his face covered with the graffiti of
scratches and welts, his eyes blackened and swollen, his
clothes mud-stained and matted with blood. The figure he
presented was of a man involved in a common thrashing,
the very image of defeat.

"I have no right to look at your little daughter. It is I
who might infect her, not Abelardo, but with a disease worse
than those bacilli of his—with my unwholesomeness."

I was so happy, that I could not share his bitterness. He
reminded me of the image I once saw in a book from my
beloved father's library, the picture of a female monkey
eating apples off a tree.

Chevalier left, but in two minutes he was back.

"You, you must be happy at all costs! And her too! For the two of you I would give my life and more . . . but I know that I can be of no use to you whatsoever. First I have to get my star out of the mud."

He left again, only to come in again immediately.

"You don't have to forgive me, nor Abelardo either. I don't deserve forgiveness. I stagger under a bellyful of toothless junk and raucous spiders."

He ran down the stairs, pursued by the shooting pains in his head. I heard him stumble and roll across the floor of the landing.

They laid you at my side; you were the greatest treasure that might be won in this world, a ray of sunshine caught and concentrated in bodily form.

The midwife drew the dirty bedclothes away from your body. I too, with the increasing ability and wisdom that I would learn from you beside me, would strive throughout your life, and for your own well-being, to separate the Water from the Fire, the gross from the subtle.

In my first dream after your birth, I dreamt that you were killing a bear with the head and paws of a gryphon. Then you dipped your net in the substance of your own body and caught a fish the color of Mercury.

50

THE PARDONABLE IMPULSES OF HIS CURIOS-
ity made Abelardo, for the third time, impatient; in order
to see you, he had the large window, the window that you
knew, installed in the wall that lay between his cottage and
our villa.

The two of us, you and I, spent the first few days in our
room. I would discreetly watch you, to free myself of my
exultation. You represented life, the living bread. You had
come to the earth to set everything aflame.

For several weeks, Chevalier disguised himself as a pen-
itent beggar.

"I have committed the most terrible sins, so I must perform the greatest penances."

He reenacted, with this, an ancestral belief which, altered
or distorted, may be found among every people and nation
of the earth. He told me that he was trying to avert super-

natural damnation, though he feared that both he and his posterity might be irredeemably damned. What comfort it would have been to him had Abelardo, in a torrent of anger, vituperated him!

"You may bury my soul between my legs to punish me for my evil intentions, and then plant onions and disappointments on top of it."

How he yearned to be purified!

"Burn me with these forceps! I deserve it!"

He hit, at last, upon the absolute madness of begging Abelardo to punish him for his running away by beating him, furiously. But how free and unaffected he would have emerged from that penance, given the ineffectualness of his friend's strength then!

I dreamt that you were already a young woman, as you would be at the age of sixteen. You were so like yourself that I tremble now in astonishment as I write this. You wore your hair long and uncombed, and you scorned frivolities and conceits. You ruled humanity thanks to a few clods of sand that lay beneath your feet. All the women who came to see you were afraid that you would bury them in that sand. They adored you because you were, for them, the Light, absolute spiritual illumination. Under your mask of indifference and serenity, you embodied, in silence, the occult Science. Your vassals and servants built a pyramid of sand for you, on which they constantly wrote your name, after every storm: "Illuminata."

51

ALTHOUGH I NEVER REPOSED ANY GREAT
esteem, much less trust, in those who might call themselves
"bureaucrats," I inscribed you in the Civil Register as my
"natural daughter." I imperturbably obeyed that legal formality, as ingenuous as it was necessary if the Law was to
accord me the rights that were mine and if I was to avert
that dark day when the State, or your progenitor, should
come to claim you and to take you away from me, as they
had done with Benjamin. You would be my daughter alone.

"Who is the father?"

As a matter of principle, public functionaries consider it
irregular or immoral that an unmarried woman should bear
a child. The Registry clerk's curiosity was not satisfied when
I replied that the father was "unknown."

"Give us the name of the man who seduced you."

The clerk thought I was trying to protect your progenitor, when in fact I was trying to protect myself from him.

"We're used to this sort of situation here. Trust us. If you tell us the man's full name, we'll find him and make him face up to his responsibilities like a man."

I was determined that I alone should be granted the rights of father and mother, so that no one would ever be able to wrest your paternity from me.

"You'll never make us believe the child was born by the grace of the holy spirit, you know."

How sordid the inquiry was becoming.

"You've got to admit sooner or later that some thoughtless bastard took advantage of your female weakness and left you like this."

I shocked him, though to no avail, when, from my propensity to speak the unsoftened truth, I pointed out to him that it would be more logical to consider the progenitor, and not me, as the victim of the advantage that had been taken.

"Do you mean to say that you were temporarily insane when this occurred, and were driven to frenzy, to blind passion?"

I shocked him even more when, in absolute serenity, I confessed that the act of your conception was the most lucid act of my life.

52

I DREAMT THAT YOU STRETCHED OUT YOUR hand to try to pick an apple from the Tree of Life. A female monkey appeared with a piece of rope and tied it to a branch of the tree, to pull it down to you. Much later, two crippled female judges crowned you with leaves, flowers, and fruit, transforming you into the image of fecund Nature. Another female monkey grabbed the Sun and tucked it into the foliage on the right side of your crown, and then grabbed the Moon and tucked it into the foliage on the left. A serpent with a human head appeared, menacingly coiled about the trunk of a fir tree.

The clerk in the Civil Registry, his short curly hair powdered with age, called me a "hot chick." He and his colleagues deplored the Law's silence with respect to this case. It was their opinion that the Law should take custody of you from me and that you should be locked up in the

Orphanage or handed over to some charitable institution. They thought it imprudent, and even dangerous, for a mother to bear a child in "irregular circumstances." They blindly insisted upon calling your conception a moral profanation. They showered on me anonymous advice that reeked rage, incivility, and gaucheness.

"I came here to inscribe my daughter in the Civil Registry, not to debate Ethics."

How that statement enraged them!

"Let's get this over with. We've had enough of your insolent pomposity. So just tell me—what name are you going to give your daughter?"

"Vulcasaïs."

"But that name's not on any list of names. It's not on any calendar of saint's days I ever heard of, either. Where the f—— did you come up with a name like that?"

In order to send many of his inane remarks to the limbo of pointless objections, I serenely explained the derivation of your name.

"The Fire enclosed in Matter, *Vulcan*, combined with Truth, *Saïs*, are the elements of my daughter's name."

"What rot. This dame is babbling."

Two nights previously, I had had a series of visions just before going to sleep: I saw you as a fountain of living water, as a woman of stone, as a celestial nymph, as a huntress provoking a magical conjunction of the heaven and the earth, and as the Path of the Wise Man leading into the Sea of the Philosophers.

53

CHEVALIER, HIS CENSORIOUSNESS LEAKING out through the mask of humility, never called you by your name.

"What a name you've hung on the poor thing; it's stiffer than a sermon and more affected than a sea urchin wearing spats."

Everyone found fault with your name; I was called grandiloquent and pretentious. I was so happy, that I never answered those who criticized me. You were the most extraordinary child in the universe! From the very first moment, how I loved you!

Yet even from the first years there had already begun to appear, darkly scattered and disguised, secret signs that foreshadowed your strange inclinations.

How anxiously I watched over your spiritual health! How smugly I congratulated myself on the astonishing rapidity with which you learned to read and write! How merited was the admiration aroused by your prodigious talent, my gifted child!

Around your fifth birthday you secretly wrote that mad and incomprehensible note that I accidentally discovered:

"Why learn Latin and Greek? What I want is to be rich and live off my investments!"

I did not question you, however, about that outrageous declaration, in which your incoherence passed all bounds.

A few days later I took you to a secondhand-book store where I experienced, redoubled, the shock of perplexity. Standing on the very tips of your toes, you were gazing at a set of reproductions of the engravings of Julien Champagne. You seemed so engrossed and intrigued that the owner of the shop came up behind you and pleasantly asked you:

"Do you like them that much?"

"Oh yes, so much."

"Do you want to buy them?"

"Of course!"

"But I'm sure you haven't the money."

"I can pay for them."

"How?"

"By selling my friend Chevalier as a slave."

54

IN SPITE OF THE FACT THAT HIS PULSE BEAT
so sluggishly that its threadiness was accounted a sure sign
of his impending death, Abelardo sketched you, on your
fifth birthday, at the knot of a sheaf of lightning bolts, as
though you were a bubble at the center of the picture. From
your figure there sprayed out a burst of lines, which represented the shining rays of a star.

Abelardo spent the winter, for the fifth time, without
stirring from his bed, swallowing draught after draught of
medication. Chevalier suspected that in secret he coughed
up blood, but that with the complicity of his nurses he
cloaked the truth. How furiously he raged one night when
he surprised Abelardo in a fit of bloody coughing!

"I am an evil beast, a monster with a poisoned soul! Last
night I poured a waterfall of vituperation over him, I stoned
him with my mineral meanness."

Heaping reproaches and complaints, all unjustified, upon his friend left Chevalier so torpid and befuddled!

"He has no idea how to take care of himself . . . nor does he show any desire to. He's growing fat upon his illness, like a duke. Not to mention that he's gaga with your daughter . . . more than he would be with his own. His eyes see rainbows in the clouds."

By the age of five you already possessed Grace. I knew that you would throw down the ancient wisdom of the wise men and the old science of the scientists. With goodness, which was the secret key, you would open the sanctum sanctorum of Nature.

"Stop daydreaming! Stop thinking that your daughter's some reincarnation of the Queen of Sheba and Tarzan of the Apes!"

Chevalier, dulled by his dreamy fantasies, would sometimes listen to me without hearing a word I said. What riches, what marvels he might have achieved had he only possessed a thimbleful of discipline! He might have put his free will and his enthusiasm to work for himself, in spite of his lack of wisdom. But he invariably took the low road, as though to prove the blood from which his disorderly nature was descended.

No oath swore you to me or me to you, ever; no precept tied us one to another; no vow or promise committed us. Only integrity, freely assumed and voluntarily obeyed, linked us.

From the first day I stopped to look at your little hands at work at the furnace in the cellar, I realized that all was well, that all things came from you and that to you all things would return.

55

TO JUDGE BY YOUR OUTWARD PROOFS, YOU possessed, from the age of five onward, the scientific and intellectual knowledge of an adult. Nature, who opens to each and all of us the door of the sanctuary of wisdom, gave you the gift of precocity. From the moment of your awakening into the knowledge of right and wrong, the consciousness of Reason, you left puerilities and trifles behind, you discovered the rudiments of the true Science, and you read the treatises of the Adepts.

I attentively studied the advice of positivistic pediatricians, rejecting no useful counsels that might be gleaned from their sectarian and exalted certainties. Following their indications, you were, by the age of five, not only a fair, upright, and charitable person but a healthy, strong, vigorous child as well, who had never been held in the intractable and obstinate clutches of childhood diseases.

"Yes, Mother."

What faith you had in me! How zealously you took up the project! The moment you learned how to read, write, and count, I initiated you into Algebra, Philosophy, History, Greek, Philology, Chemistry, and Latin.

"But woman, how can you give your daughter a logarithmic table as a present? She's going to turn out staler than the bacon off Noah's Ark."

Chevalier could not understand how you could study so untiringly, nor how you could play with the educational toys that molded your mind, nor, above all, how I could point out to you day and night the symbolic elements occult within Nature.

"You're a great ungainly philosopher-bird trying to get off the ground with your nestling and fly through some faded, gloomy sky."

Chevalier was mistaken. I led you only where it was right to lead you, and had recourse only to the philosophical tongue or the language of the gods when I judged that I could not express what I needed to say in any other way. But how right it felt to be with you!

The sulfurous genius and the mercurial genius were the nightly artifices that led you slowly, but unerringly, through your labors in the furnace. How they served, honored, and enriched you! What great goodness was yours as you romped among the stars!

56

NOT MISLED BY SUSPICION OR GUESS, MY soul had but too many occasions to observe the events: Abelardo had made contact with Benjamin by letter. How tardily I discovered this! It was Abelardo himself who informed me, when he feared the blow might come upon me from another direction.

"Please don't be distressed. These lines will tell you everything: Benjamin's agent wrote to me asking me to restore a seventeenth-century miniature he had just bought at auction. We exchanged a few letters, and then Benjamin stepped in. Our correspondence is limited solely to my professional work. I do not believe he knows who I am, or even, so far as I can determine, that my cottage sits beside your estate."

I decided never to think again about that figure that threw its shadow across us like the wake of some dark time long ago. I thought it best to keep from you that past, pregnant with frustrations, that had so disillusioned me. And yet for a few days I could not find the scarecrow that would put the flock of my memories to flight.

That night I dreamt that a winged dromedary with the muzzle of a black panther ruled the nocturnal world of the Moon. The Moon was wet, cold, and gave off silvery glints. Then a little woman-gnome with hairy hands appeared. She ruled the warm universe of the Sun. The two creatures stood beside you to watch over you and to protect the golden apples of the Garden of the Virgins.

When I woke up, I had a fleeting vision: you were like Hercules, and you were strangling and corrupting the serpents of the grave. My dreams enraged Chevalier.

"Leave her alone! Let her live as what she is—a little girl! Stop stringing rosaries of philosophical misery for her—speaking of roses, that's exactly what she's like, and she'll wither in a day if you keep on like this. And put a lid on all this new madness of yours, too, saying she's the fruit of two sperms."

How innocent Chevalier was! Although his imagination was not bad, he had but middling judgment, though a good dose of ingrained canniness. His mind could not grasp, however, the fact that there is a masculine sperm and a feminine sperm, and that they do not gush forth out of the earth, but rather out of the entrails, stemming from the operations of the four elements. It was the two, intermingled, that engendered your noble, beautiful, and immaculate body which I loved so much.

57

I HAD NOT BEEN ABLE TO ENLIST NICOLAS Trevisan, that graduate of the School of Medicine who courted me in my aunt's garden, into my cause. Nor had I succeeded in convincing the obstetrician who attended my delivery; not even the clerks in the Civil Registry would take me seriously when I went to register your birth. Your progenitor himself neither wished nor was able to understand the reasons for your coming into this world; the project appeared to him the most outrageous of nonsense. Yet, thinking solely of you and of your mission, I bore up— serene, unbending, wise, charitable, and good.

So as to be freed of the common yoke of prejudice, you were given private lessons each day by those professors least infected by contemporary fallacies and intolerant convictions. Unconsciously they made you see the relations between knowledge and the times. With flexibility I trained you to disentangle truth from error. But more firmly standing upon my objections than rendered mute by my discretion, I revealed to none of your tutors the secret purposes of my plan.

You were always taller and healthier than the other girls your age. Everyone was amazed at your tremendous intellectual abilities. Before you were six you were already reading and writing Sanskrit, Greek, Hebrew, English, and Latin. Your astonishing precocity astounded and baffled your tutors. How normal it all seemed to me! What would they have said had they known how much you were learning in secret, without the public vanity of praise?

By chance I received news that your progenitor had been imprisoned for fraud. I anxiously asked myself whether his seed, setting its poisons and perturbations in motion within your flesh, might not leave in your spirit or your body, over a long period of time, seditious traces. I rejected that uncertainty, which clouded my happiness, as absurd. How mistaken I was! I simply did not know to what degree education is incapable of eradicating the weeds of inheritance.

58

FROM THE TIME YOU WERE FIRST ABLE TO
distinguish right from wrong you would go down into the
cellar with me. How quickly and with what consummate
art you learned to attend the fire in the furnace! The technique was so luminously simple, in truth, that it required
neither professional ability nor the knack of the specialist,
in spite of the secret that attached to the process and that
could not be revealed.

How readily your attention was drawn to the unexpected
results! How easily you understand, even as a little girl, that
most of the results diverged from those predicted by the
rules of positivistic Chemistry!

How conscientiously I sought out and selected your tutor
in Chemistry! What a surprise was in store for the gentleman
I chose, when he discovered that his pupil was not yet five
years old. Since the origins of vulgar Chemistry are purely

phenomenological, our plan, by grace of the secret techniques taught by the Magisterium of the Work, lay outside the realm of its speculations. It is because of its carelessness, its oversights, and its certainties that official science has fallen into such crude depths!

You achieved the derivation of the first Quintessence at the age of seven. How ecstatically I contemplated the metal dissolved in the furnace, just as the laws of the Art decreed! You saw at once, without any explanation, how greatly that transmutation differed from the analogous operations taught you by your tutor in Chemistry! What overpowering joy that modest first step gave me! It confirmed for me my knowledge that grace, coming as a gift from heaven, lay like a celestial canopy over all your acts. Of the myriad achievements your virtue would allow you to attain, your sweetness gave me abundant proofs.

That night I dreamt that you tossed a magic wand up into the air, and when it fell into the sand a serpent and a snake coiled about it, to form the emblem of peace and reconciliation. At that very instant, Water was flung into the Fire and the waves burst into stars as witness to the union of Heaven and Earth.

How fortunate you made me feel, with your precocity and your simplicity! How certain I was, after that first victorious transmutation, that I could lead you into the Way that led in turn to the realization of the Work! How infinite was my disenchantment in the end!

59

BEFORE LATIN, YOU LEARNED ANCIENT Greek, the ancestral language of the Adepts, since with but small variations ancient Greek impregnates all living languages.

"Teach her the language of the gypsies, g——it, so she can dance as free as they do! All this stammering and sputtering Latin is going to wind up making her a sardine in a henhouse."

It exasperated Chevalier to see you writing Sanskrit or Aramaic, as though such tasks might make your little hands lose mastery, direction, and strength forever.

How early you saw that the foundations of our language are Hellenic! How you loved to turn up the relics of Greek words buried in our tongue! What a gift you had for following the clues back to the source! The Latin element of each word—how superfluous it almost always seemed to you, what a thin veneer, unable to alter the core of the word. With such satisfaction I listened to you expound your thesis to your tutor in Philology! The literal meaning of the classic texts always mattered less to you than their spirit.

"Your daughter is exceptionally gifted. Why don't you present her for her university examinations? We could get her a waiver of the age requirement."

Your knowledge did not require the absurd sanction of any institution, for it was not the spawn of obligation or of cold curiosity. At first I did not understand the menace that such frivolous remarks implied. I thought people wanted to exhibit you like some circus freak, when in fact what they were attempting to do was violate the secret of the project, break our adhesion to one another, dissolve our union, permute the pure into the impure, and prevent us from following the precepts of fiery, spiritual Nature. Those poor tutors of yours looked at us with brows wrinkled, and through a lens of the obscure uncouthness of their doubts.

Abelardo sent me a pen-and-ink drawing. It showed an eagle flying with its prey clutched in its talons, and holding a sign that read: "The Soul rises when the Matter precipitates."

60

WHEN, WITHOUT APOLOGIZING FOR HIS REV-
els in profligacy, Chevalier came to see us wearing his gro-
tesque mask, he appeared to be drunk. He had put on a
disguise and painted his eyes—how beautiful they were!—
with a dark cosmetic that looked like coal.

"It isn't coal, woman, it's kohl. A soldier brought it to
me from Africa. Smell me! Patchouli! All the perfumes of
Arabia, to excite a pup in heat."

He was talking frenziedly, but then suddenly he shifted
register, more toward the band of compassion than of chaos:

"Don't mention this to Abelardo."

With what curiosity you observed him!

"With these darling jacaranda eyes I seduced the wildest
colt I have ever known. What a stallion he is! Look at him!
He's over there waiting for me by the gate. See him?"

You did not miss a single word of Chevalier's babbling. How I wished you had been asleep!

"Yesterday our eyes met for the first time. What grandeur, like some sublime Niagara! What agony, to be sucked into its vortex! How he ignited my little tinderbox!"

I did not like Chevalier to express himself in that way in your presence. The subject he had embarked upon, I had planned to explain fully to you later.

"You are a tender butterfly, my dear, but you still have a trace of the know-it-all bookworm you hatched out of."

As you listened you grew more and more dazzled and curious.

"We ducked under the arcade in the plaza. I was melting with anticipation! When our tongues . . ."

I begged him not to recount every detail of his fall in front of you.

"But if I don't tell you, you who are my soul sister, who shall I tell?"

He rushed downstairs. He ran across the garden and disappeared with his conquest. Abelardo, unmoving, sat at his window observing the scene in silence. You said to me:

"I think, Mother, that I am beginning to guess what concupiscence is."

I put you to bed at once. Many days during that time, I thought I ought at least to explain to you how a sterile, vile, and impure body might, through the action of goodness working as a solvent, be generated, supernaturally.

61

YOU WERE BUT SEVEN WHEN, ATTACKING MY peace of mind point-blank, you told me, at last, your first dream:

"I dreamt I was born in Reims in 1503. The sun, though it still retained some of its heat, no longer gave light to the earth. My father, an officer in the King's Army, was tall and thin, with a beard and black eyes. He would often lose his temper, and he would not tolerate things that displeased him. My mother was a sweet, calm woman who was so clean that the house shone like a silver cup, but she was afraid of her own shadow."

Never, until that day, had you hurt me. As you recited your dream, showing such little emotion for such a moving story, I bore your attack unflinchingly, yet wondering whether you had invented it so you might wound, and thereby upbraid, me.

For three nights Abelardo and I sat up awaiting Chevalier's return—Abelardo shielded by the low wall of the balcony of his bedroom, curious yet fearful, and I at the window in the library, possessed of great light within my judgment.

"Mother, when is Chevalier coming back?"

Chevalier had such an appetite for chimeras! He might be rescued, but he could not rescue himself. He acted as a Guide to error, ruin, and death. How far from spirituality, perfection, and purity he dwelt!

"Is this 'man stuff,' Mother?"

With surprising second-sightedness you had a foreboding that Chevalier would return bruised and beaten.

"I can't sleep, Mother. I want to bandage his wounds when he comes back."

Suddenly you looked at me, and putting great thought into each word you said:

"Mother, in the park I noticed that boys have a little finger down there and that girls have a little thing like a bread roll."

How empty and meaningless the world seemed to me when, unwittingly, you would make me suffer. I myself felt so vile, so monstrous, so weak within the vulnerable fortress of my life.

62

THREE DAYS AFTER CHEVALIER HAD RUN
away, an ambulance brought him back, his memory obscured and his body bearing the ugly signs of an altercation.
Abelardo looked after his friend with such fervor and self-
sacrifice, lavishing upon him all the mercies and kindnesses
his desire could invent! He wrote me a note that very
morning:

"As you know, Chevalier has returned, badly injured.
His face is bruised and battered, and there are several cuts
that are infected and that I fear may grow worse. He cannot
move his left arm. He has lost his right earlobe, which looks
as though it has been bitten off. I have not asked him any
questions, nor has he offered any explanations. One would
guess that his face has been violently struck, several times,
against the floor or a wall. If you would like to see him,

come whenever you like—I will remain in my room during your visit."

During Chevalier's convalescence, Abelardo improved greatly, as though he no longer felt the sting of the desperate predictions rained upon him by the doctors. He stopped coughing, and the fever that had sapped his strength every evening abated. He no longer grew tired even when, in order to care for Chevalier, he went up and down the stairs. He seemed cured of his tuberculosis forever. But when Chevalier, after a month, was able to take his first steps in the garden, with his left arm in a sling, Abelardo, betrayed by his old ailment, relapsed. He began to cough again, his temperature rose, and he suffered a dreadful hemoptysis.

I was so sorry that Chevalier could not use his left arm. It was totally paralyzed from the cudgeling he had taken. His face little by little began to emerge from the scratches and scars, and his features began to grow more distinct. But as a reminder of those black days, his nose, with its concave profile and its slightly upturned tip, was transformed into a monstrous appurtenance flattened against his face.

"I look like one potato stacked on another."

He did in fact resemble a boxer battered by life and KO'd by fate. What a deplorable example that morass of madness and folly set you!

63

THE EXTENT OF YOUR KNOWLEDGE ASTOUND-
ed your tutors countless times.

"With what she knows, she would pass the examinations
with honors. At eight years of age!"

During those days I discovered the secret notebook in
which you would write those delirious and morbid sentences.

"What do I care if Alexander the Great was famous?—
Long live the Queen of the North Pole! —I'm going to be
shipwrecked! Olé! —I live in a supremely idiotic city.—I
am lost, deranged, furious, sick, and stupid. —I dream of
sunbathing, infinite strolls, and mad extravagances. —I began to die the second I was born. —The coffin is the *raison
d'être* of the crib."

These absurd sentences, like that incomprehensible note
you wrote at the age of five, contradicted every moral teach-
ing I had inculcated in you. I decided not to mention my

discovery to you, or even to sit down with you to examine the reasons that impelled you to write those words. I did not know whether you were sticking your tongue out at yourself, in painful mockery of the miserable fate life generally holds for mortals, or whether you were stricken with grief for the implacable fate that death deals humanity. I would have liked to be able to tell you, without betraying the secret of your notebook, that these bouts of uncertainty were the suffering that your passions and your nascent explorations required.

Sometimes more searchingly and sometimes less, there were few days that I did not ask myself whether, once you had been given the essential intellectual and scientific education, I ought not to lie down and die. I would gratefully expire, not once but a thousand times, in order to give you life over and over again, and to ensure your constant growth and vitality. At last I convinced myself that every day I died and every day you were born out of my death, reborn upon my lifeless body. How I wished that I could meet all the debts and obligations of my motherhood every day, and die for you, moments before you awakened!

I dreamt that I was looking at myself in a mirror. My face dissolved, little by little, and was transformed into the face of a crow. My body secreted an oily, greasy sweat, and emitted an odor of pestilence.

6 4

WITH PERFECT EASE AND INCREASING FRUIT-
fulness you learned to isolate in the furnace the Spiritual
Fire, materializing it in Salt. You alloyed the pure Fire,
essence of the hidden Sulfur, to the Mercury of minerals
and imperfect metals, and you did so with such exactitude!
How expertly you sought the celestial Light lost and scattered in the shadows of the Body! You knew that without
that irreplaceable light you would be able to do nothing.

How quickly and simply you learned what I had assim-
ilated only through years of study and error! With what
judicious tractableness you worked at the furnace! You
showed by that labor that you were good and charitable,
and that it was not you who wrote those violent and
pessimistic sentences scribbled in your secret notebook
but rather some diabolic creature that intermittently in-
habited you.

With what virtuosity did you induce the reaction of the first elements, Water and Fire! During the first phase, you produced Igneous Water, Common Mercury, Aqueous Fire. How skillfully you employed that solvent in preparing the Philosopher's Mercury! A voice within you whispered that one day you would arrive at that moment when, under the action of the Elemental Fire, you would attain both the first and the second Magisteria.

You listened to me with such attentiveness! It was the sign of your perfect understanding of the plan. You initiated yourself so simply and perspicaciously into the properties of Sulfur and Mercury, the prime generators of all metals.

"But then, Mother, they have to be, the two of them I mean, the origin of one unique substance."

The inquiries that initiated you into the project arose from you yourself, as the books had counseled me. These questions gave indications, and ample warning, of the brilliance that would shine from your splendid talent.

I dreamt that a chubby little girl, a sort of female Bacchus, and bearing the Bacchic thyrsus, was sitting on a huge wine vat which held not wine but Mercury. Hundreds of adults flew through the sky toward the girl. She said to them: "I am Eve, the mother of men." It was then that I realized that she had your face.

6 5

AS SOON AS CHEVALIER, MUCH IMPROVED IN
the use of his not-long-since fallen humors, came to see us,
he swore once again, as God was his witness, what I did
not ask him to promise. He feared that neither his words
nor his silences interested me.

I learned that Abelardo continued to exchange letters,
with excessive frequency and on the sly, with Benjamin.
Benjamin was now more than twenty years old. Sometimes
I wondered if he knew of your existence. I presumed that
he did not write to me because he knew I would not reply.

The recrudescence of his friend's tuberculosis annoyed
Chevalier.

"Soon he'll be nothing but skin and bones. He's a stick
of asparagus with a light veneer of transparent skin. But
where does he get the strength to cough like a brawling
teamster?"

Chevalier, without the slightest sign of commiseration, judged him. After each of his descents into debauchery it would be as though he revived in a fit of penitence only to be immediately drowned in infinite contempt for his friend. Insensibly, he found himself despising Abelardo's tribulations, mocking them mercilessly.

"He's such a tiresome bore! He wants me to be overwhelmed and embarrassed by his absence of recriminations. He doesn't even complain when I storm out of his room and slam the door so hard the needle on his gramophone jumps."

Chevalier did not like the music his friend listened to day and night.

"All that squeaky rat-music is depressing! Debussy is as dull and plodding as he is. Today I asked him whether he hadn't imagined me while I was gone wallowing in my exhaustion. You see, he knows I'm always in my best shape when I'm fagged out."

How attentively you listened to him, as though you had been snared in the snapping jaws of his hair-trigger imagination.

"He knows I have a lover's ear. He knows I can listen to the other person's breathing and hear when desire has reared its head, and that I can sense its every need. Why isn't he dying of jealousy?"

That night I dreamt that you were riding on the back of a female Colossus made of wood. The two of you were striding across the waves of an enraged ocean.

66

YOU HAD TITLED YOUR SECRET NOTEBOOK, with incredible precocity but most inauspicious promise, *Inferno*. How carefully you hid it! In it you described sentiments that I could not imagine you experiencing. They were inspired in you by some second nature residing within you, enigmatic and pathological:

"Discipline, morality, work, and goodness must be toppled with axes like old, dry trees that keep the saplings from growing."

And yet with what perseverance you studied each and every phase of the project! But in your *Inferno* you wrote haughtily and scornfully:

"I am rotting. —I worship free liberty. —I have no heart. —I am looking for a pair of ears to listen to me."

Did I not always listen to you, and most attentively? Sometimes I wondered whether I should have told you that

I knew of your secret notebook, and other times whether I should not consider that farrago of perverse and insolent babble merely a mischievous little girl's experiments in obscenity.

"I am bleeding. It's the thorn of thought."

But when you were alone with me, in the cellar, through your mask of indifference I could make out the flickering of your spiritual fire. We two kept the secret of your labors at the furnace sheltered from frivolous curiosity. One of Chevalier's pleasantries, however, may have suggested that he had guessed something of the project:

"You two are going to get your fingers burned, and your dreams are going to get all smudged."

At last I brought myself to accept the idea that in your secret notebook you unburdened yourself, you "let your hair down," so to speak, by means of fantasies of no great significance. The being that expressed itself in your *Inferno* was ruled by error; it was not you, and you hated it.

With goodness, sagacity, and perseverance I had given you the knowledge that would enable you to break free of the frivolity of the world's poor madmen who think themselves sane.

67

HOW DEEPLY, IN SPITE OF YOUR TENDER years, did you satisfy the demands of your curiosity by delving with me into Nature. How boldly you attempted to imitate Her! You would say to me:

"Yes, Mother, you're right, as always. It is only with a simple soul that one can attain wisdom."

I guided your privileged mind with countless precautions, urging you to live following Nature as a guide.

"You're going to make her swaybacked with this Percheron program of yours. Your daughter is a little girl, don't forget. You're making her live the life of a menopausal librarian with antediluvian eyeglasses."

In spite of his good intentions and the affection he bore us, Chevalier could not comprehend the breadth and import of your mission.

"Besides, I've never seen your daughter cry . . . or even laugh. That's not normal!"

He would have loved you to throw tantrums and whine like any other little girl.

All the hours of the day were not enough to carry out the project. What pleasure it gave me to see you study so tirelessly, and never to be idle! You served Wisdom and Goodness so faithfully and with such zeal! How could you one day rebel against your own destiny?

How you had longed for your triumph! From the first instant you chose the most arduous road, so that you might show the world the proper Way. How cold and indifferent you were to earthly things, to mundane glories! You always behaved with such clear, bright judiciousness!

Abelardo and Chevalier could not help you, much less accompany you. The interest they showed in you threatened to bring about confusions and imbroglios. Me, however, you understood, and how perfectly!

"Yes, Mother, I'll do as you say."

The harmony of your words calmed me. You possessed the virtue to overthrow every threat and menace.

I dreamt that a flying lioness, in fierce combat, was attacking a serpent armed with the horn of a rhinoceros. The animal's body, when the lioness had won her victory, lay in a sea of black, thick blood.

68

YOUR TUTORS, MEN OF SUCH COMMON SPHERE, taught you everything they knew, but they were unable to maintain the discretion that I had demanded of them. They spoke about you to their own professors at the University, and they divulged the secret. To our misfortune, you aroused great and unwholesome interest. You became, for them, a prodigy, a carnival sideshow phenomenon.

They insisted upon giving you the university examinations. At ten years of age, you could not waste your precious time on inane probings of that sort. With despicable wiles, however, they managed to examine you in secret, in our own villa. We were the victims of a conspiracy, an abuse of our trust, and a violation of our privacy.

When Chevalier showed me the newspaper, I had to make a great effort not to reveal my terrible displeasure.

"Have you seen the news? Honors in every subject! We have a genius in the house! I knew it. Why do you hide her away this way?"

How I feared that they would kidnap you as they had Benjamin! I made the decision, with your assent, to bar the door to our villa forever to all those savage and profane barbarians from the University. In order to draw attention to you and to destroy the plan, your tutors had made public everything that should have remained hidden.

"She reads and writes several living and dead tongues as though they were her own. —Her knowledge of Philology is exceptional. —Her talent for Chemistry and Mathematics is astonishing. —She possesses a most profound understanding of Philosophy."

From that day onward, we determined to do without those tutors who taught without pleasure or feeling, with such little judgment, and with such drudgery and vexation. You continued your education with the books of the Masters. How happy I was, choosing the readings best suited to the project, with no one's aid.

At last I convinced myself that the whirlwind of events raised by those fatuous professors from the University, with the complicity of your tutors, had in fact been a positive element in your education. We realized that we had to protect ourselves from such madness and folly, which was as arrogantly as it was obstinately pursued.

69

FOR A FEW DAYS WE REMAINED INDOORS AND secluded, feeling more comfortable alone together than in company. Chevalier, with his keen intuition, realized that I did not want to see him, and he left us alone. Abelardo sent me a drawing of a brilliant star. Underneath, he had written this legend:

"May this be the true sign that your daughter, like a pilgrim, has successfully reached the end of her first voyage."

What tenderness, what thankfulness I felt toward him! He had read my heart and realized how deep my anguish had been during those painful incidents with the University.

For the first time, you took the initiative in replying to him. You drew him a flower of wisdom, and titled it *Rosa hermetica*.

The next day, at last, we went out into the garden and

we saw Abelardo through the window in the wall. He smiled sweetly.

To make amends for the insults to which the University had subjected me, Chevalier bought me a book by Raymond Lully, an antique edition of *The Book of the Friend and Beloved*. I opened the book at random and I read:

"164. 'Say, madman, what disposition most strongly draws thee: loving or hating?' I replied that it was loving, for I hated so that I might love."

The time had come for you to learn the mysteries buried in the loins. I myself taught you the reproductive systems of the various animal species, of vegetable life, and of humankind. I informed you in great depth about the medical, sociological, and philosophical aspects of procreation. I regaled your curiosity with a wealth of knowledge from that chapter of life—a chapter from which Chevalier had already imparted to you so many, and such macabre, indiscretions. In this subject, as in all the others, you quickly expressed yourself as a free and judicious individual, with goodness and deliberation.

After your tutors had stopped coming to our villa, how happily you worked in the cellar! We set ourselves at the service of our fate, against whose decrees no one may revolt.

70

HOW EARLY YOU BECAME A WOMAN! UNDER
the sign of the Sun, you worked at the furnace with your
girlish little hands. How expert they were! You consecrated
to the Work the most excellent of your gifts. With justice
and equanimity I listened in rapt concentration, the confi-
dante of your most private self, as you commented aloud
and pensively upon your work in the cellar.

"Mother, the stone has turned saffron-colored, and yet it
weighs and looks like pulverized glass."

How skillfully, how quickly you grasped the essence of
the project. The secret language of the Adepts was your
true mother tongue; I spoke it but as a foreigner might.
Your speed, your precision, and your intelligence made me
proud, and filled me with wonder. Each time you worked
at the furnace I had the impression that you were illuminated

by an inextinguishable light that flowed from an eternal lamp.

You did not, in truth, learn the Art. From the very beginning, it was within you. With what simplicity and dexterity you performed it! The union of the body and the soul of metals concerned you less than the condensation and agglomeration of the soul under one coherent, firm, and refractive nature. With what gravity and wisdom you succeeded in sheathing and impregnating each stage of this union, assuring thereby the efficacy and perfection of the plan. I wondered whether you fully grasped the universality and essence of the agent. While they were yet in their nascent form, you skillfully manipulated the insensible metals, which lacked any vital capacity of their own. Watching you, only with difficulty could I control the desire that I suddenly felt, to weep with happiness!

"In appearance, Mother, these metals are dead. That's why it's impossible for me to extract the potential, latent life from the depths of their solid, crystalline mass."

Your face lit by the red-hot coals of the furnace scrutinized the fusion so keenly! How lovely you were! How concentrated you looked! A child, yet with the form of a woman filled with every virtue! And how sensible, how wise! How straightway you found the Path in the midst of that tortuous Labyrinth!

71

TWO ENGLISH SCIENTISTS, HAVELOCK ELLIS and Herbert George Wells, neither keeping nor respecting that severe and natural silence that is proper to true Science, wasted their time and ours in trying to begin a correspondence with you. More than by their letters, which we left unanswered, I was annoyed by their remarks to the newspapers. How many words they used, to say so little! They wanted to write you, and even to see you; your precocity astonished them, they said over and over again, as though that had any weight or bearing on the matter. Professor Wells, the more offensively familiar of the two, wanted to exhibit you at a congress in London.

With astounding arrogance Benjamin at last wrote me, offering all sorts of aid and spattering us with droplets of advice. To perfect yourself, he said, you ought to go live in London. With infinite brazenness and even greater hubris, he proposed to foot the expenses, since, he said, if he had enjoyed great success, the reason lay in his leaving his natal country. What an ungrateful wretch! Neither my beloved father's love nor my own lessons any longer entered, for him, into the causes of his success. Naturally, I did not allow myself the slightest relaxation from my labors in order to reply to him.

You were now traveling so far, and without even stepping out the door of the villa! At the furnace your journey now loomed long, dangerous, uncertain—and vain if you should stumble or make the slightest false step. Well might the ship have sunk upon its maiden voyage. You sought to orient it, navigating with judgment, struggling ceaselessly against sickness. You might grow nauseated, and vomit behind the door, and yet what peerless indication of the sought-for dissolving that sulfurous vomit always was.

"Mother, I see a unique black color, and all the earth dry and split."

After that first of Benjamin's missives arrived from London, you said to me with an intensity that considerably outstripped your usual calm state:

"The Sun and the Moon are eclipsed in unison. I see them as pure allegories."

72

YOUR SECRET NOTEBOOK CONTINUED TO BE A
field for weeds and thistles. How fittingly you had named
it *Inferno*! It was a proper place for Angels of Darkness and
Beelzebubs.

"I went out walking with a herring hidden under my
skirt. —I will be a rebel to the marrow, and I will stink!
—I will defeat order. —I am so nauseating!"

How alarmed and distressed I was to discover an old
skirt of yours that stank of rotten fish! With Chevalier as
your second, you had gone out wearing it, unbeknownst
to me.

"Let her be, let her go out walking however she likes.
And if she feels like it, let her dress up as a sardine with
measles. Here she's always covered with lace and feathers,
like some duchess in her gloomy garden."

You became so unlike yourself when you went out with

Chevalier! He told me everything one day, as though it were all nothing but childish pranks:

"How she loves to shock the prudes! When your daughter goes out with me, she's another person. What fun she is, and such venom she has inside!"

When you wrote in your notebook, you seemed governed by those same harsh inclinations:

"Die, pusillanimous cowards! —I'll shoo them off like they were no better than 36,000 newborn poodle pups!"

Neither Chevalier nor I appeared in your *Inferno*. But indirectly, you may have alluded to me in this paragraph:

"I live at the expense of another. Cynically. —I am the princess of filth. —I invent the mangiest, most despicable, basest, and most cretinous of actions and words. I am paid for that with scientific books. —I shall never, never work. I will be on a constant slowdown strike. —My sad and lonely heart drools."

In the cellar, you contradicted the barbarity of your words with your devotion to your exhausting work. You worked at the furnace with such zeal! How studiously you read and reread the books of the Adepts! The prose of your secret notebook might mislead me, but my eyes could not be fooled when with them I watched you, a thousand times, stand modest and indefatigable in the furnace's brilliant glow. Contemplating you, I was washed clean of the mildew of excess and adulation, and I shone forth with every sign of purest admiration.

7 3

ONE NIGHT, TO CROWN YOUR LABORS AT THE furnace, you uttered a most bizarre question:

"Mother, what's the total price of the fuel and materials needed for the Work?"

The price was as infinitesimal as the Magisterium was rich and copious. How many hours did you spend locked in the cellar at night, working on the project!

"Mother, look carefully at this substance. It is a book, too."

And such a book! The waferlike crystals of that mineral, whose peculiar configuration resembled mica, lay one upon another like the pages of a book.

How easy it was for you to extract the inward Fire from Iron, rousing it with shocks and friction. Iron is, to the naked eye, that metallic substance in which may be found the greatest proportion of the latent sputtering Light.

Wrapped in a long cloak, Abelardo spent six weeks in the garden restoring three medallions. How patiently and meticulously he brought them back to life! At noon, Chevalier would wake in a fury. A hangover pushed his ill humor to the brink of desperation. And turning his back on forbearance, he made Abelardo bitterly pay:

"You're worse than some fusty old maid! Can you never stop working, as though you were some slavish bee? I'm sure you got up with the birds this morning, to earn our daily bread with those tireless little brushes of yours. Have you discovered perpetual motion? You're dying to tell me that you're the poor hardworking little ant and I'm the shamelessly good-for-nothing lazy bum of a grasshopper. Admit that you despise me."

At the first shot of the skirmish, Abelardo would stop painting, as though it would have been impolite to listen with brushes cocked. Hours later, Chevalier, fawning, would give him a long, slow massage, rub the back of his neck, trying to patch things up after his petulant outbursts.

"With these wizardly fingers of mine I can magically remove the headache that I myself gave you with that philippic of mine. What a man you got stuck with! Such luck, you poor bugger!"

7 4

THE CHANCELLOR OF THE UNIVERSITY, AS though given license and leave to indulge his deliriums, sent us a letter so utterly absurd! He gave you permission, at twelve years of age, to begin whatever course of study at the University most attracted you. How shamelessly, how brazenly he burst into your life, without invitation or by-your-leave.

I dreamt that you were floating in the center of a pool, and that you wore the body of a mermaid as a sign of peace and unity. At the edge of the pool there was a bustling group of hunchbacked and deformed princesses. They were shinnying up gigantic horns and throwing stones at you. They were making horrible faces which disfigured them even more. Just as you were about to die from the stoning, there appeared on the horizon three queens, bearing the attributes of magic, and with white hair, and they saved you.

The Academy of Moral and Political Science begged you to give two public lectures. Four political parties tried to enlist you in their ranks. What laughable bids they made, as though your time might be sold at public auction! I was worried that some little man possessed by an evil spirit, and dressed from head to toe in the cassock of ire, should recognize you when you went out.

Stung by my silence, the faculty of the University wrote me a long letter filled with affectation. They were oh so infatuated with the fanciful idea of giving you lessons by correspondence! And so insistent about giving you a written baccalaureate examination there in the villa, as their colleagues had done for the university examinations! What buffoons they were! Chevalier lent himself to the farce:

"Why don't you let her take the Law examinations, purely out of curiosity? If the child became a pettifogger, she'd lead all those judges by the nose!"

How frivolous and inane it would have been for you to squander your time and energy with professors who pretended to climb as high as their wildest ambitions goaded them!

By your twelfth birthday, after a decade of study and labor, you had achieved the knowledge of an Adept. How proud of you I was!

75

ABELARDO INFUSED PHLEGM INTO MY BLOOD by sending me, by Chevalier, a sheet of pasteboard on which he had drawn a combat between an eagle and a lioness. The combat took place against the background of an open book. On the back, the figure bore a brief explanation:

"You are right to oppose the University's breaching the peace in which you and your daughter live. The academic world will never be able to understand that which is supernatural in her. University education cannot penetrate the true Mysteries."

A few days later, he drew a secret, silent, and profound nocturnal landscape. In the center of the firmament there gleamed a supernova, an immense glowing orb composed of thousands of celestial stars. He had added this saying in India ink:

"That luminous guide, the Universe, is the modest ally of Wisdom."

Abelardo offered so many and such varied symbols to Chevalier! They were received, however, as proof of his friend's misanthropy, not of his spirituality. What scowls Chevalier shot at his friend's eyes, and what insults he threw in his face! Such grumbling rage he showed!

"His mind goes in more circles than a greased top. And he's older than Methuselah, besides. It's not blood in his veins, it's turnip juice, and watered down at that."

He threw a dark cloud over those qualities most superior in Abelardo, his discretion and his modesty. He would have preferred Abelardo petulant.

"I swear, even if he didn't have consumption he wouldn't go on sprees with me. He's a taciturn chameleon that only gets really carried away by melancholy."

Chevalier once again was spending nights out. At dusk, Abelardo, whose mildness of spirit made him kneel at his friend's feet, would spruce up Chevalier, using his brushes to paint his face and eyes, tracing his eyebrows and brightening his lips, and infinitely pampering him.

76

FROM THE TIME YOU WERE TWELVE, YOU alone, without any help of mine, would keep the fire of the wheel and watch over it. With what painstaking care did you sit in vigil at the furnace, knowing that any interruption of the firing would have entailed the loss of the materials. Suckled upon the milk of the Magisterium, you were an active child, yet one of great attachment.

How quickly you learned, by your own quick wit, to control the furnace's combustion! How skillfully you prevented the temperature from falling! With what precision did you feed the fire when it reached the transcendental state! You knew that any accident would have meant the loss of so much time, even if the project itself was not fatally compromised.

With what wisdom and good sense you avoided excesses!

You could gauge the process as though you possessed some intuitive thermometer.

When the amalgam was at red heat, the merest breath of calcination would inspire you to regenerate it by dissolving it once again. How judiciously you refired it! Watching you, I stood in awe. Already I had spent so many years of repose and happiness!

"Mother, how long did it take the Adepts to achieve the Work? How many years did they spend working at the furnace?"

That question—so senseless!—surprised me so much! It was not worthy of you. The months of work, the years, the decades, perhaps an entire lifetime, should pass without distress or intranquility. Haste, or the contemplation of profit, might annihilate the project forever. That childish impatience of yours happily never tormented you again.

With such mastery did you divide the Earth from the Fire, the gross from the subtle! You separated without destroying. How profitably you received the virtue of the superior things and the virtue of the inferior things.

I dreamt so many times that you climbed from the earth to the sky and then came down to be beside me, roaming free and happy.

In the cellar there always lay, unlit, a lantern with its shutter half open. Its unlit wick spoke of the dangers of those who, working, are seized by fits of impatience and become greedy, or fickle, or hungry for novelty.

77

YOU BEGAN TO APPRECIATE THE BENEFITS of Science at an age judged by philosophers, artists, and Adepts to be premature. How readily had your persevering studies, combined with your work in the cellar, shaped you into a new woman, a being unique in all the world! Those victories brought great elation to my soul, and filled it with happiness and fortune.

"Yes, Mother."

With dedication and tenacity you proved the truth of the Magisterium. You received, without any aid of mine, the initiation passed on by the writings of the Adepts; I could only be a spectator—but what a fortunate spectator!—of the process.

"Yes, Mother."

Benjamin had taken such a different path! Music had immediately offered tangible, public benefits to him. You, on the contrary, worked as assiduously as you worked silently. Benjamin traveled the world, without the slightest shackle on his haughtiness, reaping trivial triumphs, while you, renouncing the world, a voluntary recluse, carried the project to its fulfillment. Benjamin forgot the role I played in his childhood; you were good, upright, and above all grateful.

"Yes, Mother."

How grieved and hurt I was by the noxious correspondence between Abelardo and Benjamin. I refused to ask Abelardo to put an end to that unhealthy relationship. I could have done so, and should have. How different everything between you and me would have been! In the most indiscreet way Benjamin, from the shadows, snooped on our lives and meddled in your future.

Chevalier read the letters and, generously, tried to justify a person unworthy of that defense, though without first performing a rigorous examination of Benjamin's heart by standing in the presence of his bitter and crotchety acerbities.

"That Benjamin of yours, it's as though he's been beaten to a pulp—spiritually, I mean. He's traumatized—you can tell from his letters. It's as though somebody had whipped his soul and left it in bleeding tatters. His mother is a venerable w—— and you know it, and *you*, you won't answer his letters. Nobody knows who his father is, and he wakes up to find himself orphaned from a mother to boot. Parentless on both sides of the ledger."

78

HOW MANY TIMES, READING YOUR SECRET notebook, did I ask myself whether you were foundering in madness among the shoals of two contradictory personalities, and in fact whether you were not rowing blindly toward the rocks of schizophrenia. I never made the slightest allusion to your *Inferno*, so that I would not be guilty of worsening the split of your mind into two opposed natures.

"Fate has made me seditious. —I corrupt all my emotions and I become horrible. —Beauty, goodness, science: what meaningless, ignominious words. —The unknown is going to barrel around the corner at full tilt. —My disobedient soul grows depraved."

How it gratified me to watch you, so poised and placid, after I had read those disconcerting words spat into your secret notebook like gobs of spittle. You worked at the furnace with such discipline and obedience! What pores on your lovely cherubic face did those terrible black storm clouds issue from?

"I have a louse farm on my head. —I throw them at the mothers in the park and at their little nurslings."

Trees began to appear with inscriptions carved by you, with a razor, into their bark. It seemed that this new phase signified an advance in the development of your disorder.

"Die, books! Down with Science!"

How little your phrases meant, how much they tried to say! But I never openly criticized your *Inferno* in any way.

"I descend to the depths of drunkenness. No one understands me, nor ever will. —I, she's somebody else."

And yet how good you were, in spite of all! With what demanding faithfulness to Science did you work at the furnace. You forged for yourself discipline and obedience, so that you might arrive at the infinite wonders of the ineffable Arcana. You approached beauty, as the dreamt-of model of grace.

79

CHEVALIER CONTINUED TO GO OUT AT night, netting adventures of all sorts in his way. He would return, never alone, in the wee hours of the morning. The farewells to his companions were invariably tricked out in insults, shouts, and blows.

How solicitously, each evening, Abelardo would prepare Chevalier for his nocturnal revels. Chevalier, like some blushing bride, would grow warm without any outward spur; he would sit patient, though very talkative, until the moment he left us; his desires would constantly break out into fantasies.

"One must have fun! And not like Abelardo, who's as shriveled up as a dried-out prune. And that, of course, is contagious, as everyone knows. I have to treat my body to a body."

He left as dolled up and natty as he came back wrinkled and tawdry.

One day, Chevalier brought an artilleryman back and took him into his room. They spent the night brawling, trading insults, and laughing. The next day, they sat together in the garden as they took breakfast. As the two of them billed and cooed shamelessly, Abelardo, all humility, buttered their toast. With what avid curiosity you viewed that scene!

When the soldier had gone, Chevalier, enraged, turned upon Abelardo.

"You did that on purpose! You ruined my party out of pure jealousy! How twisted you are! It kills you that I've got a friend like him, admit it. You're an envious wretch and an ingrate."

Abelardo began to cough, and suddenly he raised his handkerchief to his mouth. He filled it with blood.

"I've had it up to here with all of your subversive tricks! And now we are asked to witness the melodramatic spectacle of a handkerchief full of bloody sputum. What you want, and you may as well admit it, is for me to feel guilty and for everybody to cluck and call you a martyr, when the only person who's got a right to cough up his heart through his mouth, out of sheer frustration, is me."

Abelardo, locked within his pain, tried to control himself, but he could not prevent a violent fit of coughing, and then another stream of blood.

80

I NEVER LEARNED HOW THAT PHOTOGRAPH of you, printed on the first page of the newspaper, came into their hands. How frivolous and inexact the article's snips and scraps of nonsense were! And how humiliating for the two of us. They dished up with lies what they'd never have dared serve as truth. They invented such nonsense as that you had agreed to take the baccalaureate examinations and that you admired Nietzsche, La Salle, and Kautski.

With equal respect for the truth, they announced that you were to give an address in the bullring. We were outraged by their interminable and indiscreet meddling in our affairs. The Center for Social Research contacted the Austrian doctor Sigmund Freud when it was reported that he had become interested in your case.

I hired two gardeners to guard the villa, with orders to forbid entrance to everyone, without exception. How I feared a repetition, with you this time as victim, of that unhappy episode that my beloved father and I had lived through with Benjamin!

On the sly, Abelardo answered the letters written him by Professor H. G. Wells, sending him tidbits of our lives by post. How shamelessly he betrayed me! When he discovered that I had guessed his deception, he gave me as a gift two Roman coins, attempting to pay the price of his betrayal with pieces of gold.

"How happy I am to know that you have finally learned that the eminent English scholar H. G. Wells has written me several letters during these last few weeks. I must acknowledge that I have replied with honesty and discretion to all his inquiries about your daughter. I have been hoping that I could tell you this modest secret. Allow me to confess to you that all the attempts I have made to discover your true personality have been so far in vain. They have only revealed my own vanity. You are, to me, as invisible as you are mysterious."

Abelardo, through the fog of his partiality, thought that I willfully hid myself in the presence of goodness. How difficult I found it, indeed, to cling to goodness so as not to feel myself cheapened by his disloyalty!

81

HOW WOUNDED WERE MY EYES AND MY SENSE
by the foolish claim you committed to your secret notebook:

"I demand legal and sexual equality."

How I would have liked to be able to ask you about the
scope of your petition. Did you ask for equality as a girl
among adults? as a human being within Nature? Those
sudden bouts of madness that ravaged you when you were
all alone, how terribly they afflicted me.

A few hours later, in the cellar, I was very moved when
you told me in that good-little-girl's voice of yours:

"Mother, envy and injustice will never destroy the modest
fortune I have amassed with the Magisterium."

You expressed yourself with the uprightness of an Initiate. How perfectly and accurately you chose your words!
How tellingly you formulated ideas!

"I worship all the knowledge I possess, Mother, and venerate it as an honored gift of Nature."

In truth the fruit of your labor at the furnace was a wondrous gift, but so were the food you ate and the liquids you drank. You grew so steadily and honestly that every day I was taken aback in wonder. Such uncommon wisdom resided within you! When you stood at my side you gave witness to such a profound and mysterious gaiety! How I shared with you in your excitement, when your happiness reached its peak in serenity and order!

Even when you spied upon the intense moments of intimacy between Chevalier and Abelardo, you never lost your exemplary tranquility.

Chevalier demanded that Abelardo paint a portrait, a nude, of a friend of Chevalier's; it was to be in imitation of Jean Grossart's *Adam*. When the painting was finished, Abelardo wrote upon it, with no outpouring of reprehension, the amorous dedication that Chevalier had composed for his new friend.

That night I dreamt that the burning coals were at last consumed, and that the furnace grew cold, while you sang an aria in an unknown tongue.

82

I DREAMT THAT YOU WERE IMMORTAL, AND that you stood hieratically before a dry tree with lopped-off branches and pulled-up roots. The tree was floating majestically above the ground. A female gladiator with a sword split a beehive in two without being assailed by the swarm of angry bees. The honey spilled out slowly and gently and flowed in a stream to your feet.

A few weeks before your birth cut short my impatience, I had the furnace, in the shape of a hexagonal pyramid, built; at it you would perform such wonders. The two doors, set face-to-face, would give you access to the hearth. You would handle the tools with the dexterity and speed of an Oriental doing calculations upon an abacus.

You observed the phases of the Work with such penetration as you peered through the two glass ports! Through a ventilation shaft you evacuated the gases that were produced by the combustion, and you did so with such masterful control that you gave proof thereby of the excellence of your goodness.

How expertly you built the nest within the furnace! In the burning sand you then proceeded to the incubation, for which you employed a metal bowl. You concentrated so deeply through every operation that you spoke not one word to me.

By your thirteenth birthday you surpassed me by such lengths that I became not your disciple but your admirer. You could learn nothing from me, for I had nothing more to teach you. My pride was never more stirred than when I, as sole witness, stood and simply watched you at your labors.

You conceived natural, occult Fire as the immortal agent of all relationships. With this sacred Fire you would unleash all the metamorphoses of Matter. How many decades the Adepts had to work in order to achieve the perfect alliance of ability and energy that had already dawned in you, at thirteen years of age!

83

HOW MUCH GOSSIP FLEW LONDON-WARD
folded secretly in the letters from Abelardo to Benjamin!
What a deafening buzz of falsehood, and how plagued with
giddiness and confusion! Every week they wrote one another, as though meddling in our lives were a duty. Sometimes Abelardo recounted to me certain of Benjamin's
indiscretions. How unhealthy and perverted a thing his curiosity was, and how degrading for us! I knew him perfectly
capable of arriving unannounced at our villa as though it
were his own home.

Benjamin was the protagonist in an ancient tragedy on
which, for your own good, I had long ago rung down the
curtain. And yet you were so intrigued by it that one night
you asked me to tell you the old story. Out of sheer caprice
you were flirting with chaos, and you caused me deep grief,
while you, in turn, contemplated with sangfroid the abyss

into which your curiosity led you to peep. How vexed I was by that betrayal of your wisdom and discretion. Devoured by curiosity, and unheeding of the counsels of good sense, you were bamboozled by whim, folly, and the urge to pry.

I showed you the chasm that separated you from him. I had set Benjamin upon a path that in my ignorance I had thought was the perfect one. It was a baroque road, without perspective, and with no final end but conspicuousness. I neither initiated him nor could have done so, for I was then unconscious of the occult and mysterious meaning concealed behind Nature's expressions. I fell with him into a sea of darkness far removed from eternal wisdom. How little interest that insipid event of my younger years should have aroused in you.

That night I dreamt that you were sailing in a boat, zigzagging through the waves. The sand of the desert carpeted the ship's deck. You left the wheel to plant bones at the foot of a fir tree that was rooted in the foredeck.

Your self-knowledge, in spite of the guile and perverseness that sometimes took possession of you, grew greater every day. Thanks to this self-knowledge, you were unceasingly purifying your goodness, modesty, and simplicity, the principal virtues of a soul as advanced as yours.

8 4

"I AM BUT A PEDESTRIAN. —SEVENTY-THREE secretaries with lead eyeshades surround me. —I am the base, inept, stubborn, low-life passerby. —I will answer with silence those who interrogate me."

You never gave me back silence in answer; on the contrary, you replied to me in the most sensible, prudent, penetrating way.

Over my deeds, your respect and your affection imposed their virtuous sway.

"Yes, Mother, you're right."

But in your *Inferno* you would write words swollen with insubordination, rank conceits of arrogance.

"I will howl like a she-wolf soon. —I will be the most wretched and despicable lycanthrope, the most dangerous werewolf."

How those fits of obscenity stung me! From the highest reaches of morality to which one had seen you climb, now to have descended to such shameful outbursts! Wallowing in those obscure signs, yet without your brain being in the least jangled or discomposed, you touched the lowest depths of opprobrium.

"I will be happy only in degradation and violence. — For reasons of hygiene I will destroy all that passes for beautiful. —I will sleep with the wicked. —I will nourish myself on the filth of the dung heap."

The transcendental cause, the proximate reasons, and the consequences of your excrementitious words were an enigma, and enigmatic were the reasons that led you, with such convulsions, to squeeze the pus out of your infected soul.

Two oaks, planted in the same year, were growing in the garden. One was as vigorous as the other was frail. How different were the stars that inexorably guided their two unequal destinies! The strong tree symbolized mineral vitality, and the weak one, metallic inertia.

You yourself grafted, upon your upright nature, a wild shoot, and it was that which provoked your second personality, that personality whose slime oozed from the insolent mouth of your pencil, and which so wounded me when I read the funereal messages you wrote in your *Inferno*. And yet I not only respected you, I admired you with all my soul.

85

SHORTLY AFTER YOUR FIFTEENTH BIRTH-
day, Chevalier disappeared for two weeks. Day and night,
Abelardo, burning with anxiety, waited for him. Wrapped
tightly in his cloak, he spent fifteen days stationed at the
garden gate, and at the threshold of despair. Chevalier had
announced his departure, but not precisely how long he
would be gone, passing off as childish neglect what was in
fact the purest premeditation. You watched it all in silence.

"Don't wait up for me. I'm going to spend the night—
and longer!—like a wild she-goat with a hermit. I need a
change of air. Abelardo smells of shadow, and I can't breathe.
I can't live like some widower dressed in gray leaden crepe."

Chevalier demanded that his friend perfume him and
paint his face. With tender care Abelardo indulgently
combed his hair, exaggerating its waves; he brilliantined his

hair, sprayed it, and tied it up. When he was at last scrubbed and polished, Chevalier exclaimed:

"With that part on the right, I look—imperial! I need it. I have to raise the flag, and the lather."

When he expressed himself so ornately and with such elaborate tropes, he betrayed his agitation, rather than impressing us with the refinement and subtlety of his language. How sad it made me to see him so carefully coifed and nattily dressed, when all one saw on his face were the scars from his last row. He had taken off the sling that had held his injured arm; how much worse it was to see him like some wounded veteran of the war incapable of moving his paralyzed limb.

"I'm going to have as much fun as a centipede with a millipede. I've made that very clear to Abelardo. This time I'll have no self-deception. He has to know that I'm bored with him, so he can really demand nothing of me. It's enough that I tolerate him. The most infuriating thing of all is that he doesn't say a word, but I know he's got one of those green-eyed monsters inside him, eating at his entrails like a worm."

You knew, though the others, the common run of mortals, did not, that Gold opens all closed doors, such as in the furnace.

86

LACKING EVEN A PASSING ACQUAINTANCE
with our intentions, people felt free to speculate on the
outrageous and unfounded rumor that you had offered a
challenge to the university authorities. It was said that you
had agreed to take their examinations. You were the talk
of the idle and the itch of the busybodies. They were all in
a rush to exhibit you, as though you were some parakeet
that knew how to add and subtract. How impatient they all
were to corrupt you, according you no greater honors or
epitaphs than hubbub and hurly-burly.

Your presence was requested upon the most motley and
least appropriate stages. You were ideal, according to every
spontaneous organizer who came along, for talks, confer-
ences, debates, sermons, and most of all for political rallies.
To hear them, one would think that you had been an acolyte
in every church, member of every union, militant in every

party, votary of every sect, and volunteer in every army. All the correspondence went directly to the bottom of the wastepaper basket.

The Professor of Logic at the University submitted for your consideration an indecorous questionnaire which I, in concern for your peace of mind, did not show you. The man intended to employ your replies to compose a book titled *Sexual Rebellion in the Young.* He wrote you an outrageous and futile letter in which he constantly spoke of the sort of lewd and indecent temporal problems generally consigned to the compost heap.

For the first time in my life, I wrote, in faithful adherence to my inspiration, a brief literary piece:

"*Sky* liked adventure. One day he saw *Flame.* He wanted to take her for his prisoner, and to do this he thwarted her husband's vigilance by making a shower of gold fall upon her. Nine months later, *Flame* gave birth to a son, *Red Sea Fish. Chaos, Flame*'s father, enraged, locked the mother and son into a trunk and threw it in the sea. Sailors fished up the trunk and gave it, with the mother and son still inside, to the *King.* The *King* did not free *Flame* and *Red Sea Fish,* but rather sent them to the *Land of the Wise Men,* where they lived the rest of their lives performing miracles. *Sky* was punished by the *King*; he was transformed into rain for all eternity."

87

IN THOSE TWO WEEKS OF CHEVALIER'S absence, what an insistent and tedious drizzle of pain there was! Abelardo, wet to the bones with grief, could find no refuge under the eaves of consolation.

Two days before Chevalier's disappearance, Abelardo sent me a watercolor. On a naked scimitar there were drawn four erect flowers of four different colors. Each bore a sign, written in Gothic script: the black flower bore the legend "Time"; the white flower, "Grace"; the yellow one, "Union"; and the red one, "Foundation." On the back of the watercolor, Abelardo sent me a compliment that flattered his hopes:

"I have the presentiment that soon I will be well. It is an irrational premonition, for I am experiencing no improvement whatever in my illness. When I am well, we will at last stop seeing one another through the window in the garden wall, and will be able to converse vis-à-vis. Believe me when I say that I am dying of impatience."

And yet during the long absence of Chevalier we could hear Abelardo cough even more than customarily, as though his life fled him in all directions. How often he filled his handkerchiefs with blood!

I contemplated the watercolor so long that I came to entertain the wild fancy of burning the drawing of the four flowers. Suddenly I grasped the secret message that the drawing held—a message so hidden that not even Abelardo himself, in conveying it with his own brushes, had been able to decipher it. It signified that if, out of hurry or impatience, you rushed the stages of the project, you would bring about the irremediable destruction of the Work.

One morning as Abelardo read Benjamin's weekly letter he hid himself under his cloak, as though he feared that in spite of the distance between us I might make out what it contained. How all those secrets distressed me!

I bore the deceptions as long as Nature required me to. With perseverance and faith I observed all the oracles, predictions, and omens. I did it all for you, indenturing myself to the difficult science of silence and endurance.

That night I dreamt of a prison of dirty glass. In the center of it there was an abandoned tower that touched the sky, and it was filled with elephants. The King and Queen walked over to open the door, but they could not do it. Suddenly you arrived, riding in a tiny castle with wheels. You ripped off the hinges, and the door of the prison fell with a great noise.

88

WHEN YOU WERE FIFTEEN, THE HEAD OF A
little angel crowned your womanly body. The expressive
features of a young maiden—how well they covered the
luxuriant maturity that had grown strong upon the tree of
wisdom, a ripeness in which there was no trace of imper-
tinent idleness or of ill-employed curiosity.

One night I dreamt that you were an old woman with
the features of a young girl. With what astonishing agility
you towed along the Cubic Stone, which floated upon the
waves of the ocean.

How constantly and how profoundly, sustained by faith,
did you progress! Without faith, futility would have rendered vain all your vast knowledge. How sternly you re-
pelled every attack of skepticism. You knew that with doubts
you could never forge anything stable, noble, and lasting.

We are not all the same, and what immense dissimilarities existed between other people and you!

By virtue of your exhaustive knowledge of superficial, positivistic Chemistry, you could better grasp the fearful mystery of the project, which went so contrary to materialist models. Your mind would be set spinning, your reason would grow clouded, your logic would stagger backward when you observed, in awe, the infinite enigmas that Nature showed you.

In the cellar, you would spend the nights working as though you dwelt in another world. As though Youth, Glory, and Beauty danced around you in a ring, you were so happy and so good! On two occasions I dreamt that you were the flower of flowers. You shone like fire as you stood on the deck of a ghostly ship. A great dolphin swam alongside, at the surface of the sea, to escort you.

Words of joy would spring to my mind when I watched you perform wonders in the furnace. Impetuous delight would take possession of my senses.

Although years or even decades might pass before you came into possession of the perfect and tangible proof of the Work, how decisively you advanced, and how filled with grace! And yet, how many threats of our destruction hung over us without my divining them.

Why did you betray me, awaking all that should have remained asleep?

89

HOW OFTEN YOU WOULD WITHDRAW INTO
yourself as you played the piano, extracting all the forgotten
juices from the substance of the musical compositions. Benjamin, who so resembled you, would unravel the notes of
the scores with no thought of their aesthetics; his way lay
through the thicket of routine, and he took it with misgiving
and timidity. His interpretations showed skill; yours, so
unique, evidenced peace and harmony.

Benjamin was always so ungrateful! He learned the piano
to please my beloved father and me. I could never have
imagined that he could play before our enemies at the Conservatory with the same energy and fire. He was but eight
years old when he astonished those usurpers who kidnapped
him, tearing him from our lives. It was so easy for him to
accustom himself to our absence. But you, without me, could

not live. Nature had created us the fingers of one hand. I admired you so, and so rightly.

In one of his letters to Abelardo, Benjamin dared declare that I stood as an obstacle to your welfare. He wanted to help you, he said, when in truth he insulted you; he called you a prisoner, and me little less than a jailer. I had sacrificed so much for him, even knowing that I would never receive the slightest sign of gratitude from him. His arrogance prevented him from considering, modestly and logically, the nature of the project you were engaged upon, a project so different from his own!

Benjamin hounded us, unconsciously betraying his evil intentions. At twenty-seven, he betrayed his immaturity by that sick and fevered desire to come to know you, to intrude himself into your life. With what pomp and ostentation he recruited a circle of foreign luminaries, so that he might invade our villa and sweep away everything that we had created. He was incapable of seeing that he was motivated by nothing but jealousy and a disquieted soul. How envious he was of you! And how rightly so! His only pleasures were the backslappings and engaging grimaces of celebrity.

90

WHAT SHARP AND SPIKY HANDWRITING YOU
employed in your secret notebook to prick out those wild,
incoherent, and needle-sharp phrases! How distinct that
handwriting was from your usual quick, intelligent, and
symmetrical hand. Those chaotic scrawls and scratches that
were the thread out of which you embroidered your insolent
and lewd declarations—how they made my heart shrivel!
It could not be you who was the author of such barbarities
but some invisible twin sister who crouched on all fours in
the most hidden recesses of your nature.

"The work is more remote from me than a fingernail is
from the eye. —F——intelligence. —Sh——."

Seven times you repeated that ugly word "sh——." I
never surprised you in the act of secretly writing your *Inferno*. I did not even try.

"I will direct the irrational disorder of all the senses.

—When the moment comes when I have to love, I will fall madly in love with some utterly despicable pig. —It is my duty to fall passionately in love with that which is most repugnant."

How frail and defenseless you stood, in spite of your prodigious intellect and your luminous goodness! Those phrases were inspired in you by your raving Siamese twin, and I wondered if that rebellious double that you sheltered inside the most secret parts of your body might not die only with the last exhalations of your own breath.

"I will always be a rebel and an outlaw. —F—— Nature and all creation."

The deafening violence of those harsh obscenities bewildered me. You had never spoken them, and yet suddenly they resounded in the pages of your secret notebook like a string of firecrackers. I wondered whether Chevalier had taught them to you, out of pure frivolity, and without realizing the commotion their excrementitious stridencies would cause.

When you were with me you always expressed yourself in fair, chastened, and simple terms. Your fervent, precise vocabulary allowed you to formulate your ideas in the most transparently plain and direct way. You so greatly respected and honored truth that your happiness could not imagine vainglory.

91

EARLY ONE MORNING THE HARSH AND DIS-
sonant siren of an ambulance woke, and startled, us all. The
piercing sound announced the return of Chevalier; he had
been injured. Abelardo asked the attendants to put Chevalier
in Chevalier's old room on the upper floor, while Abelardo
himself stayed on the ground floor.

The dogmatic uncertainties of doctors and nurses—from
the very beginning how they dispirited us! Chevalier lay in
his bed, his body disfigured by fractures and dislocations of
bones, and covered from head to foot with bruises, welts,
and bloody scabs. But what tormented him most was the
terrible blow he had received to the knee. A horribly painful
tumor had formed, and he was immobilized. What a martyrdom it was for him even to perform his physical neces-
sities.

Abelardo took charge of everything, displaying a sudden activity as unstopping and unreserved as it was unwonted. Effortlessly and tirelessly he went up and down the stairs, which only days before would have exhausted him. We no longer heard him coughing. How transfigured he was! Cheerfully he remarked to Chevalier's male nurses:

"Don't bother to look for the people who are guilty of this. I'm certain he brought it all on himself."

He spoke loudly, knowing that his friend could hear him. Chevalier, abashed, closed his eyes and accepted the accusation in silence.

The morning on which Chevalier was immobilized by his injuries and consigned to his bed of pain, Abelardo began to lie in the sun, arms and legs delightedly akimbo, and bask. He ate more than ever, and with such good appetite that he began at once to put on flesh.

When Chevalier's wounds had been attended to by his male nurses, the doctors encoffined him in a cast. He suffered greatly, but he did not complain. The broken bones began to knit and to give him less pain, and scar tissue began to form over the wounds, but the inflammation of his tumorous knee grew, unremittingly, worse and worse, and the pain rankled as though that torment might be the only memory that remained of Chevalier, save his ashes, in the world.

I dreamt that Abelardo was living with a woman who represented the Golden Age in the innocence of the Garden of Earthly Delights. Her face was so familiar to me! And yet I could not recognize her.

92

ONLY TWELVE DAYS BEFORE YOUR SIX-
teenth birthday, I received the most insulting anonymous
letter! It was the first of several; after this missive, unsigned
threats arrived every day. Awe and admiration had cut
down the briars and brambles of the sinuous path toward
meeting you, and a high road to irrational hatred had been
opened.

Since your life was in danger, I bought a revolver with
which to protect you.

In view of all that, and intending to calm overwrought
spirits, we at last agreed that you would receive the Faculty
of the University in our villa. Muddied and beshat by their
filthy canons, they examined you. I felt so sorry for them.
Intellectually they were so inferior to you. They gave you a
series of titles, degrees, and sheepskins, which we, together,
burned on the following day, so that no ugly scar or stigma

from that absurd event, at which you had captivated the admiration of the University, should remain.

The Professor of Philosophy put a long list of questions to you, all as indiscreet and indecent as they were vapid and inane. But you replied with your habitual modesty and reserve. Under the pretext of learning your opinion of the work of Havelock Ellis, how vulgarly he queried you about prostitution, carnal coupling, and venereal diseases.

That same Havelock Ellis it was who had sent us an incoherent and interminable letter. He portrayed himself to you as an adherent of Eugenics. How insolently he pretended to give you advice, even when his admonitions were so useless and sterile. The Sexual Reform League was scandalized when it learned that you had not replied; it declared that it was my fault, since I never left you alone and since, therefore, you always obeyed my wishes. How pleased they would have been had we argued and so come to a parting of the ways.

I dreamt that Providence came to you as a goddess with two faces. The face before was that of a pure young girl, and the face behind was that of a grave and majestic old woman. As you trod down a serpent that slithered between her feet, you laid across her shoulders a philosopher's cape.

93

DAY BY DAY CHEVALIER RUSTED AND STIFF-
ened, the lineaments of his vigor little by little obliterated.
The tumor on his knee and the gnawings of his remorse
paralyzed him, while at the same time Abelardo, as though
by magic, was quickly recovering his health. How secret
and how exemplary were the causes that brought about his
cure!

Up until the day of his leaving, Chevalier, euphoric, had
been the intrepid mountain-climber to life's every Everest.
His ambitions were exceeded only by the impossibility of
attaining the summits that he sought. He would vacillate
and debate so laggingly that his energies at last would flow
languidly back once again and find their level.

"You know what a sad state Chevalier is in. I will do
everything in my power to help him bear his pain."

How moved I was by affection and pitying compassion as I beheld Chevalier in the garden on that first day Abelardo brought him down in a wheel-chair! How harrowed his face had become in that dramatic and bloody row! His silhouette was a flayed and disfigured bulk. That barbarous confrontation had brought him face-to-face with his final destiny. He was only now emerging from the struggle of darkness and confusion in which he had been living up until then. He spent his days like some stone, immobile and disillusioned. How he reminded me of my beloved father, letting himself die, come what might, like a man in despair more than dumbstruck by surprise or shock, when Benjamin left forever.

Abelardo had recovered an unwonted energy, as though his friend's ruin were but the accident that marked the end of a cycle. The mutation of Abelardo's substance marked a sinking, a destruction of a stage in his past, as plague and famine and natural cataclysm mark stages in History. But you looked so silently upon the two friends, as though you knew nothing whatever of suffering! And yet how wonderfully your mercy shone forth!

That night I dreamt that you were riding horseback with a bow in one hand and an arrow in the other. Beside you rode a chimera, a mythical beast with the body of a lioness, the tail of a serpent, and three heads. How easily you roped it, on the gallop.

94

SITTING ON YOUR STOOL BESIDE THE FUR-
nace, how fragile you looked, and how touched I was to see
you! You studied the phases of the project with a concentration so childlike, in spite of your sixteen years, yet at the
same time with such good sense and maturity.

You could not explain the obscure mechanism of the
project. But how artfully and with what grace you foresaw
and averted those things that might have led you to disaster!
And how bravely you withstood the ambushes that lay in
wait to turn aside your zeal! How often, and how absorbedly,
I watched your eyes, your mouth, and your fingers as you
worked!

You redoubled precautions and prudent care when there
appeared, floating on the surface of the liquid, the first
coagulation of the stone, so oily and so light. How precisely
you gauged the intensity of the flame so that that wispy film

would delicately break into fragments! Anxious and admiring, I watched your meticulous work. How expertly you melded the fragments back together, until at last, animated by a rotation of your wrist, they became as thick and heavy as a lump!

I bequeathed to you all my knowledge, a tiny fragment of the wisdom you possessed as though by grace. I initiated you with all the modesty of a woman who, while being your mother, knew herself to be your own daughter. I transmitted to you the entire inventory of the scientific knowledge of the age. But you knew that that framework could not support the True Science. You received the spiritual light from our common mother, Nature, through an act of revelation.

How skillfully, with what purity of technique and inborn dexterity, you put in practice the simple formulas that brought under one sole yoke the artifices of the laboratory, so that the synthesis of minerals might take place. Those first steps—what vigils, frights, and moments of keen watchfulness they had cost you! But they permitted you at last to leap into sublime knowledge.

One afternoon I saw the dove of Noah's Ark, in full flight, with an olive branch in its beak. As it passed over me, it dropped a tear of white liquid. I tasted it in such joy! It was in truth a drop of the immortal milk of the birds. I felt so blessed by that presage, a presage of such purity!

95

IN SPITE OF ALL, I SHOULD HAVE REPLIED to Benjamin's letters, if only to tell him, with an easy conscience, less beaten down and more firmly, that we needed absolutely nothing from him. I saw too late my error. He was always so stubborn! How many times, out of pure pigheadedness, had he thrown tantrums as a child.

It was the sheer whim of a celebrity that led him to intervene through a side door in your life and so, obliquely, in mine. He dreamt of ruining your mission, scattering the fruits of your labor. He conspired to intrigue several foreign personages such as H. G. Wells, Sigmund Freud, and Havelock Ellis with what he called "your case." He so infected Abelardo with his mania that Abelardo, behind my back, became his confidant. At last I discovered that he had created some meddling commission whose purpose was to root around in our lives, and to report on us.

I dreamt that a pianist wearing a sling threw seven stones at a great boulder that sat in the middle of the sea. Your face was beautifully sculpted on the rock. The seven stones bounced off the relief that portrayed you and hit the pianist in the face.

When I realized that those strangers were attempting to capture your spirit and dissolve it, I suggested to you that you should be nourished only by yourself, and that you should raise your energy and your knowledge to an even higher plane. In that way you would become irreducible and invulnerable.

Your wisdom was so dazzling that in the eyes of the world you passed from being admirable to being enviable. Benjamin and his foreign rioters were captivated only by the vain wonders. They were lured by theories as sensationalistic as they were hollow. They were utter strangers to charity.

You were not, as Benjamin, the feeblest of your admirers, said, a genius, a supernally gifted young woman, but rather, and above all, a magisterially wise one, and the possessor of consummate abilities. How dazzling was the light you threw into the darkness of the world in which we lived. You shone like a perpetual flame.

96

ENVY SOWED THE SEEDS OF CALUMNY, AND
what stubborn roots it had! There were those who declared,
cynically, that they had seen you sitting like a hussy, legs
spread, smoking a clay pipe. Others, still more shameless,
told that you sat, stark naked, writing, in the embrasure of
an open window. The gardeners also rushed to add to the
snowball of lies and rumors that was rolling downhill like
an avalanche against your reputation. You yourself, in your
secret notebook, slashed at yourself, and wounded yourself
with insults and spiritual mutilations. With what grief I
read the outpourings of arrogance with which you filled
your *Inferno*:

"F——science. —Long live confusion! —I lie naked,
and covered with lice, in the sun. —I will do whatever is
forbidden."

I never forbade you anything. Never, ever! Your free will sustained the armature of the project, by strengthening its essence. Your freedom was Fire and Sulfur, the governess of all mutations, the Incombustible Seed that nothing can consume, and the precious catalyst of the Work.

"I will live alone. Forever. Without family. —I will keep silent, given that I can only explain myself in the languages I have learned. —I will be slothful and brutish."

You were on the path to immortality, yet you wrote as though your soul could be infected by evil, terrified by death. You gushed energy and health at every joint and pore, yet you expressed yourself as though you were already experiencing the pains of agony and death. In fact, the sword with which you slashed at yourself in your *Inferno* and the trowel you employed to apply the balms and unguents at the furnace held the same substance. You possessed the double power of enervating and regenerating, of destroying and organizing.

You were never cowed by the heat of the furnace nor by the dregs of the coal nor by the danger of unknown reactions nor by insomnia nor by intense physical labor. I could not see the mirages evoked, like castles in the air, by a superficial reading of your words. The properties and virtues of your two contrary natures were melded into one original matter. You engendered the dialogue between adversity and harmony, and to what profit!

97

ABELARDO BEGAN TO VISIT US AS SOON AS he realized that he was cured, putting off the trembling of disease and discouragement and putting on joyful well-being and smiling promises. How transfigured he was! His health returned, his skeletal body filled out in but a very few days.

Chevalier grew thinner with each passing day, as though some Procrustean torturer were stretching him out to meet death. He waned—alone, afflicted, and enfeebled—upon his wheel-chair. As he feared he might bother us, he carefully measured his complaints.

"I have a horrible pain in my knee. It's as though I'd had a red-hot nail driven into me. Spasms of pain clatter up and down my bones, from my ankle to the crown of my head, and I feel like my soul is being ripped in two."

The doctors who were treating Chevalier had diagnosed a tumor on his knee and had advised that the leg be amputated. Abelardo looked after him, yet contemplated his decline with curious insouciance.

Whenever Chevalier so much as moved a finger, his suffering redoubled in flares of shooting pain.

"Doesn't it shock you to see how thin I am? I look like the backbone of a fish with all the bones stripped off. Whenever I move, this bed of torture flays the skin off my backbone and my a———. I don't sleep at night."

The tumorous swelling on his knee wobbled and quivered like some enormous melon. We attempted to make him eat, but food of any kind was repugnant to him. Fever and pain writhed in his brain like a nest of maggots, and he raved in delirium.

"How miserable I am! How wretched is my life! Why do I go on living?"

Abelardo succored his friend with inexplicable good humor. His unaccustomed optimism, more inopportune than counterproductive, made it seem that he veritably skipped.

"There's no call to be pessimistic. All diseases can be cured given time enough and proper care."

You knew that the person who eats the apples of the Tree of Science finds her soul enlightened by the honors and satisfactions of the Truth.

98

AGREEING TO SUBMIT TO THOSE OBTUSE UNI-
versity examinations in the villa—what a crass error it was!
We demanded the strictest discretion but the Faculty, in
frank abuse of our trust, improvised a rally at our very
doorstep. The crowd snorted and pawed the ground in impatience, awaiting the signal that would give them leave to
break into our lives and destroy everything we had built
throughout our long years of study and charity.

With what pompousness the Chancellor, a superficial and
vain man, drew himself up—he stood upon his rear legs
like some trained mule!

He lauded your culture, calling it "prodigious and en-
cyclopedic." He extolled the "originality of your ideas" with
the same aplomb with which he pretended to understand
them. He declared, without proof, that you enjoyed "great
and universal prestige." He affectedly pontificated that you

had already received "all the intellectual education that was available" to you in our villa. He predicted, pedantically, that in the future you would come up against "insurmountable obstacles to the self-enrichment of your exceptional mind." He announced that he was going to "create a commission of the world's most distinguished scholars" in order to aid in your education. In veiled but no less brazen words, he criticized me, showing thereby the wig with which he covered his false science.

They dreamt of hooking you, of recruiting you into their positivistic flock. The most arrogant sort of proselytism assailed your ears. That cloying fog of incense was but a smokescreen for their firm resolve to break down your resistance. Your knowledge slashed rents in their hollow beliefs and spilled their substanceless stuffing; it rendered their insipid methods null. That is why they attempted to draw you into their guild, though at the risk that once you were one of them you would lose the light that illuminated your soul.

The night of the rally I dreamt that you stood in the center of an open-air theater, dressed as a wild-animal trainer. Through a trapdoor there slithered a menacing serpent. You stared at it fixedly, and you made it bite its own tail, so that it formed a circle, the symbol of equilibrium, harmony, unity, and affinity. In the center of the circle you placed a sign that read: "Friendship."

99

ABELARDO HAD LIVED FOR YEARS ON THE verge of the grave. After Chevalier's accident, Abelardo's life was swept up in tides of ceaseless activity. He went out every day. How much time you wasted with him, tossed about by that surf! How worried I began to be about that sudden wave that had come along and thrown you overboard, into the presence of a man you thought of as a father. The truth is that given the gulf that divided you, he could comfortably have been your grandfather.

How many times I wondered whether you sat down with him to read Benjamin's letters, and whether the two of you replied to the inquiries of the curious from abroad. What tales were invented behind my back!

Pain visited Chevalier with obsessions and paranoid fits of delirium, and rendered his rest even more filled with fear, more excited and confused.

"Don't ever betray me, ever. I beg you by all that is sacred. Above all, in the state of health I'm in now, don't report me to the Army."

Chevalier's mind was possessed by the *idée fixe*, which he could not dismiss, that the Army was going to arrest him as a deserter, for not having performed his military service.

"Don't anybody call me Chevalier in the presence of the nurses. Say my name is Aden. The military authorities are capable of throwing me into prison in a dungeon, even if I'm crippled. Don't betray me, I beg you."

I too, though for different reasons, felt so entangled in betrayals, so anxious and sleepless over the traps laid by unfaithfulness!

I dreamt that a dolphin, the living image of uneasiness and worry, twined itself about an axis of stability represented by a ship's anchor. The two symbols heralded the universal Deluge. The Earth, in triumphing over Water, was emerging under the figure of Diana.

From the moment Chevalier had begun to waste away with pain, Abelardo had become so expansive! He continued to care for Chevalier, but with so little tenderness and perseverance!

100

SO MANY DOUBTS AROSE AS THE PROJECT
took its most promising path! You would spend the night,
as you always did, working, with quick eye, in the cellar,
but how often did you become engulfed in your illusions—
absorbed, distracted, and sunk in stupor.

Your abilities shrank, and your good judgment shriveled.
You stole profundity from your virtues, and the fruits of
your work diminished. Your energy no longer achieved the
same potency of transmission. How often I would see you
with Abelardo! How many whole afternoons you passed
with him! How much time I spent noting his broad influence! How soon you began to dote upon pride and preten-
sion, to the detriment of good judgment! Your fatuousness
at this time made you so conceited that it became hard for
you to put off vanity and emptiness and sit upon the stool

beside the furnace! And yet your vigor had always been your purest flame.

You tried to imprison your soul, so free, inside your body, as though in an iron chest. One day I surprised you sitting before a mirror and contemplating, for the first time in your life, your ephemeral body, which would one day return to dust. You put out the fine flame of your modesty, unconscious of the fact that by so doing you were ruining the project once and for all.

And yet at night, beside me, you would sit at the furnace and work with almost the same resolve as you had shown before. It was as though you possessed a Body for base work and a Soul for honorable and true employment.

But as soon as you took up the Work, the dark and lowering clouds above me would open and admiration would shine through. You would carry out the labors of the project with such art that the occult operations would seem to execute themselves. I loved you with such passion!

One night before you went to bed you said to me:

"Mother, so long as I can still breathe, I hope."

I got up later and went to your room, still somewhat troubled by doubt. You were not there. With what sadness the sudden thought came to me that for a few hours you had become, though fleetingly, a slave.

101

HOW OFFHANDEDLY YOU TOLD ME THAT YOU
had spent the night talking to Abelardo. You lacked the will
to give a straightforward explanation for such a long absence.
I pictured you with Abelardo, reading and rereading the
letters that came from abroad. Abelardo had greatly mended
in body, growing fat, but a still greater alteration had occurred in his sentiments, for he had the gall to say to me:

"Havelock Ellis only wants what's best for your daughter.
He is a modern sexologist, with universal prestige. And
besides, he is a specialist in Eugenics. Benjamin sees him
often, and admires him. Ellis advises that your daughter
should go to England, in order to pursue her studies. You
should not oppose this."

I could not recognize in this man who reproved me in
this way the loyal and reserved Abelardo I had known for

so many years. Chevalier's illness and Abelardo's own cure had altered his judgment.

"If you have no objection, I myself can accompany your daughter on this journey."

That powder flash of presumptuousness blinded me for a few seconds. Abelardo had wittingly descended to the level of Benjamin. The two of them, occupying the lowest station of the low, were now equals in cowardice and methods alike.

"In England, she will find, at last, a setting in which she can finish her education."

Your education, as Abelardo knew very well, could be pursued only in the villa. Science, wisdom, judgment, experience, and learning would flow into you, as by osmosis, as you labored in the cellar.

"Chevalier has so little time left! He doesn't even know when I go out anymore. God grant he not suffer too greatly or too long in this dreadful agony that is taking him from the world."

How cheerfully Abelardo prepared, indirectly, to abandon his friend.

That night, working in the cellar, you suffered for the first time the Trial by Fire. How expressively your burned hand symbolized the sacrifice and rebirth demanded by the project.

102

HOW GRIEVOUS AND UNPLEASANT IT WAS
for me to read the hail of sharp words in your secret
notebook:

"Wretchedness, aberration—abomination—hatred are
the treasures in which I have invested all my pleasures.
—I laugh like an imbecile. —I feed upon lies."

Abelardo, Benjamin, the Faculty of the University, and
all those foreign professors hounded you, and annoyed and
disgusted me. I sallied out alone in your defense, and I told
you that all things were bought with pain; but they used
such soft and honeyed soap on you, and fed you such sur-
feiting and indigestible praise, that your senses were at last
atrophied. That is why you wrote more and more foolish
and foolhardy things in your *Inferno*:

"I fatten myself on opprobrium. —I love lies; better yet,
I adore them as though they were a god. —I will bathe in

the blood of the recently murdered. —I belong to the race of those who whistle while they torture."

Abelardo dressed you up in clothes so ordinary! When I saw you so bloated and puffy in that clumsy froth of organdy, you reminded me of my sister, Lulú. That is why I said to you:

"I would rather see you dead than see you descend into spiritual abjection. You have a mission in life to complete."

Dressed in that disguise of a woman you were not, you looked at me, and you drew yourself up so imperiously!

"I never forget that, Mother. Nor that I am the one who must decide what my path will be."

We argued for the first time. Your arrogance petrified me! Your conceited airs were so suffocating to me that I thought I was about to be asphyxiated. I locked myself in my room, chilled and shivering with shock. I asked myself whether it was too late for you to emerge safe and sane from such a dreadful experience. I myself had unconsciously prepared you for it.

I considered the possibility that this sudden shameful turn might lead you, when all was said and done, to reflect upon error. I was convinced that you could still return to goodness.

103

THE SURGEONS AMPUTATED CHEVALIER'S leg, though without injury to his pain, which, in unremitting spasms, ascended into the stump redoubled. How he suffered! And yet Abelardo spent so much time with you that he neglected his friend. How sorry I felt for Chevalier! My compassion put an end to the solitude in which he had been plunged by the negligence of Abelardo. I spent so many hours listening to his groans of pain and his complaints.

"Never let them amputate a leg of yours. I would rather have died in the operating room. My suffering grows worse by the hour. I am battered and bruised inside. The leg they cut off tortures me; they did not cut away the pain."

I cared for him as though he were a child, wiping the sweat from his brow, feeding him spoonfuls of soup.

"Abelardo has forgotten me completely. Yesterday I think I heard him laugh at me. Besides, he spends the livelong day with that daughter of yours. What can they talk about? Tell me—does he have any idea how much I'm suffering?"

Other times he would withdraw into a bitter silence from which he would only emerge gasping and panting, crying out curses and incoherencies. Neither the salves nor the medication that was prescribed for him brought him any relief.

"No one in all the history of humanity has ever suffered as I do. There has to be some treatment I could take to rid me of this pain. Electricity maybe. You have to try to find out. Don't tell Abelardo that I cry. Don't leave me alone!"

How many times he screamed for death to come and take him! Sometimes he threatened to strangle himself.

Meanwhile, Abelardo and you never ceased your gossiping. Your voices would waft in, phantasmagorically, to us.

The night Chevalier's life came to an end he told me, in broken gasps, a bizarre story about the tusks of African elephants. He drowsed for a minute, lingering among the living; the violent racking of his torture at last ended his sad earthly life, and he died in my arms with a rictus of pain that disfigured his soul.

104

THE NIGHT CHEVALIER DIED, I DREAMT THAT a very robust woman with two horns on her head came up to me, an elephant at her side. When she was two steps from my bed, another woman appeared, balancing a tortoise on her head and carrying a glass of water in her right hand and a pair of red-hot pliers in her left. The first woman extracted a grandfather clock from beneath her skirt; the clock had only one hand. The two women looked at me fixedly until I woke up.

You were sitting beside my bed looking at me fixedly, like the two women who had voyaged through my dream. You smiled at me and I forgot your latest outbursts, which still echoed in my ears.

I told you my dream, disarranging it and inventing the white lie that the glass contained "permanent water," which unlike other liquids does not wet the hands.

"Forgive me, Mother, for the things I said to you yesterday."

In your infinite goodness, you found the simple, natural means by which to console me. In an instant, I loved you more than ever. Your sympathy and affection, now reborn, could subject everything around you to your will. Life emitted hurrahs and bravos, and my soul soared in slow ascension toward the heaven of purity.

Your goodness, restored, permeated me so deeply! It flowed into me through the air, the earth, and the water, as though my life throbbed and palpitated with your strength!

I had always been puzzled by the obstinacy of the men of positivistic science. They could not see that only goodness can bring about the memorable accident of the union of Science and Soul, and much less could they understand that goodness generates and maintains goodness.

"Yes, Mother."

How venial and slight my enemies became when you loved me!

105

HOW UNITED, HOW FULLY ONE WE HAD LIVED
for fifteen years! You were sixteen when, without an atom
of wisdom, you joined with Abelardo in that union. I wish
I could have told you that in spite of his apparent homo-
geneity he harbored two opposed and contradictory natures.
With what clarity I had observed him during Chevalier's
illness and death: there were two alternating, and distinct,
Abelardos. The first one, you and I loved and admired for
his infinite patience and resignation; the second—a sour,
acidic creature!—had distilled every caustic, mordant virtue,
and volatilized away all modesty.

In his last bout of delirium, Chevalier proclaimed that
he wanted to take a ship and go off, alone, to Abyssinia, as
though Abelardo had ceased to exist for him. He dreamt of
becoming rich, and of covering the walls of his house with
gold. Abelardo did not even listen. How reserved he was

in his remarks on the care I lavished on his friend until his death:

"Your dedication satisfies your desire to sacrifice yourself, but it comes too late for poor Chevalier."

Abelardo was not spurred by his friend's death to declare his grief, or perhaps even to feel it. He was now concerned only with you.

"Allow me to tell you that you keep your daughter too much out of the world. Let her travel, let her become acquainted with the world, let her live freely."

How obstinately Abelardo attempted to turn you aside, into the narrow alley that led to that Republic of Foreign Scholars, as though from dry dead trees you could breathe air of the slightest vitality. In the villa and only in the villa could you achieve perfect equilibrium. Tempered by the frigidity of the air, the heat from the furnace brought balance to your life, as Earth neutralizes the wetness of Water.

I dreamt that Chevalier, in his dying moments, wore a crown upon his brow. He was smiling from within a transparent sphere. Suddenly his soul, reincarnated in the figure of an angel, ascended, until it reached a morning star that burned in the firmament beside a tree covered with fruit.

106

MOMENTS BEFORE HE DIED, CHEVALIER, IN terrible agony, suffered a stroke of lucidity:

"I am going to die without ever seeing you give your daughter a kiss. And I have spent sixteen years with the two of you."

I loved you so much that I banished all extravagances and trifles of affection. Such foolish displays would have kept me from admiring you. I was always so happy with you! We were so good!

When I watched you work at the furnace, standing so erect, overcoming every obstacle, I would be filled with joy and happiness. When I watched you pace as though you were entering into the deep forest of hieroglyphics of the Long Way, how proud I was! When I saw you, enlightened by learning, preparing the Matter in the center of the Labyrinth, I felt myself to be the most blessed creature on the face of the earth.

Abelardo's pernicious influence forced you to retrace your steps over the Path you had followed with so much wisdom, certainty, and perseverance. Wandering in the Labyrinth, you had dropped that Ariadne's thread that would have allowed you to bring the synthetic unification to material existence.

I dreamt that in the sand of the beach you were drawing the Labyrinth of Solomon with three entrances but no exit. In the air, hanging from a cloud, there floated a starfish. Above it, in the sky, four inverted fields represented Celestial Agriculture. There shone sheaves of Gold and seeds of Sulfur, drenched with Mercury.

During those days when I was so troubled and vexed by you, I could not forget how many gifts you had given me in the past. The volcanic rock of turmoil, arrhythmia, and imbalance enclosed the impenetrable secret of that terrible decomposition of yours.

I told you that you were in danger. You looked at me as though I were mad, and you laughed. You had never done anything of the sort before.

107

WHEN I DISCOVERED THAT BENJAMIN HAD arrived in our city, I felt a stab so deep and an anxiety so troubling! He took a room in the Hotel Ritz, and Abelardo immediately went, with you, to visit him. I never learned what the two of you spoke about the first time you met, or whether you spoke of me. Abelardo told me that there had arrived with Benjamin a biologist "of noble lineage" who had fallen in love with you. He made jokes about a subject that would bear no frivolity:

"We need to get that daughter of yours married off!"

That bizarre assumption lay outside the province of the project. Your energy, at such folly, would experience an irreparable loss of substance. Your will and your knowledge could only continue to exist in close embrace with your soul. Your evolution and the progress you had achieved showed the goodness and rightness of your labor. Benjamin and

Abelardo, like Attila's horses, dreamt of laying our land waste.

Your fate, unique in all the world, could not bear additions, alterations, and rearrangements. Abelardo, however, had pretensions as an architect:

"Your daughter is no longer a child, she is a woman. And entirely so! In comparison to other girls her age, she is much advanced in every way. It's natural that she should feel an attraction toward the opposite sex."

I always loathed vice and evil-mindedness. How many men and women of genius had been lost when they met that hydra-headed beast. You could not associate yourself with base matter and abandon your sense of mission on this earth. Abelardo spoke of "falling in love" without any eye to its morbose and degrading consequences.

Your mission presupposed the fusion of Soul and Nature. Your persevering studies and your labor at the furnace had enabled you to raise your intelligence to such a degree that you understood the inapprehensible. You shone like a star, a martyr, an industrious virgin, and an immortal. Nothing and no one could discourage me!

108

AT THE HOTEL RITZ, BENJAMIN SERVED AS host to a gaggle of scholars who had just come over from England in order to fasten upon and usurp your will. Abelardo, like some mendicant with his hand held out for praise, served as their go-between. Hanging out your life—and mine—in the light of shameful public examination, they stared at you as though you were some queer bird.

How I would have liked to forbid you to go out with Abelardo, but how much more that you, of your own accord, should have refused to accompany him. You spent whole afternoons with them, and you returned so faded and changed! Then, at night, how distracted you seemed.

During your absences I would read and reread the frightening sentences scrawled in your secret notebook, but which you had stopped writing since Benjamin's arrival:

"I have poison in my blood. —I will bury honesty.

—Who dares oppose me, when I am the most evil of all?
—I have the aftertaste of ashes in my mouth."

Abelardo turned up the volume of his vituperations, accusing me of governing your whole life.

"I assure you that you are going to exhaust your daughter's patience."

How irremediably alone I felt when I heard those unfair reproaches and those inane and vacuous counsels. He had never spoken to me so emphatically.

"You are going to weary her with your megalomania and your obsession to control and dominate her. You don't let her breathe."

Abelardo had erased from his memory the fact that you were born as a product of my all-encompassing will to see you fulfill, for your own good, the loveliest and fairest mission one could undertake.

"One morning your daughter is going to wake up and say *Enough!—I want to live my own life, without your control.* Believe me, I am telling you this for your own good."

I dreamt that a furious tempest beat against a fragile, crystalline rock, threatening to shatter it and scatter its pieces into the sea. But two cherubim blew their breath over the waves and calmed the storm.

109

I REMEMBER AS THOUGH IT WERE YESTERDAY
the last time you worked at the furnace. Absorbed in your
manipulations, you possessed all the beauty of a daughter
of Science.

With what artfulness you burnished, under the influence
of the fire, the whiteness of the matter. Gradually, however,
you managed to bring the mass, which was acquiring the
shape of a perfect lunar disk, to a lemon-yellow color at its
surface. Both sweetly and with a note of rivalry you said
to me:

"Mother, I have the sensation that I totally fill the round
universe. Look how the matter has reached its ideal state of
dryness and stability."

This sign proved that you had reached the attainment of
the first phase. How fortunate you made me feel! Those
men of science who had dragged Benjamin over from

England in order to corrupt you—they could not even imagine the things of which you were capable.

With what infinite care you recommenced the operations to augment the power and virtue of the matter. I was so dazzled as I contemplated you that last time you worked at the furnace! You offered me that night a happiness complete.

A joyous delight penetrated me at that eternal instant which preceded saturation, yet so subtle was my joy that it could not take body in emotion. It shone out into the darkness with unparalleled intensity, though it did not echo in my living heart. I was dissolved by it and, through you, into myself.

For years Abelardo's humble devotion kept alive my affection and my admiration for him. His beautiful friendship with Chevalier commanded praise. But from the moment his friend died, he was changed into a base procurer, and placed himself at the service of our enemies. He traded pity, mercy, sympathy, for a bubble. He did not know that my indissoluble union with you was the necessary requisite for your harmony. How fertile and blessed we might have been had we been able to live together always!

110

NO ONE WILL EVER IMAGINE WHAT TERRIBLE
pain I suffered the last week of your life.

From his hotel room in the Ritz, Benjamin led a cam-
paign to incite all the famous men of science to mutiny. He
would attempt to destroy your tranquility in the face of
tempests, your contempt of worldly gratifications, your serenity, your stoicism.

I learned too late that Benjamin's pack of scholars had
given you a series of examinations as degrading as they were
inane. Abelardo, with mad purpose and patent censoriousness, cheered on the assault enthusiastically. He malevolently
celebrated the irreparable consequences of those degenerate
tests.

"Your daughter is supremely gifted, a genius unique in
history. The men of science who have examined her, men
who hobnob with the luminaries of the world, are still

astonished. You cannot let her rot in some corner out of the sheer jealousy of an abusive mother. You cannot suffocate her within the four walls of your house. If you do not let her live her life, you will be committing a crime against Science."

They wanted to turn you into some parroting schoolgirl; they were trying to disturb your mind. They dreamt of imprisoning you in some research center so that you could generate, as though you were some mere seed, another being. Their hubris knew no bounds; they imagined that that "other being" would be wiser even than you. What they were in reality trying to do was exploit your learning. If you had abandoned the project to follow them, you would have lost your vital energy, your independence, your power, and your freedom. The ineffable Light that bathed you was only accessible to the Pure. Of you, those men knew only the husk of the husk.

That night I dreamt that an old lady of yesterday was transformed into a young girl of tomorrow. The vanished, lost, and wandering people of the world came to her. At the end of the dream, the young girl revived the dead.

111

WHEN I REALIZED THAT I HAD FAILED AS A mother, I thought I would go mad. So much energy expended for so many years, threatened to be turned to ashes.

How often during those days I thought of suicide! The revolver I had bought to protect you could end, with one blow, one brief bang, my days.

That first time that you confronted me, I was on the point of throwing myself from the roof of the villa so that I would fall to my death on the terrace below. I felt so utterly defeated! You had brutally fled from the Light into the Darkness, from radiant Quintessence into Chaos.

Instead of imitating the simplicity of Nature like a good artist, what vain chimeras you pursued! Thrust roughly into grief, I realized that you wanted to go off to England to enchain yourself to some vile man.

After a week of silence you announced to me:

"These are the last days we will spend together, Mother. I'm leaving. I'm going to travel and to live my life freely."

I heard your voice, but it was as though another person were speaking to me. I stammered out some meaningless phrases in reply. If the pain had not obscured my reason, I would have pointed out to you that the Seed requires its proper ground in which to germinate, grow, and bear fruit.

"You're mistaken, Mother. No one is trying to corrupt me."

You were rushing toward the abyss, toward weakening and waste, toward impatience, toward activity without respite or repose. How you disappointed me!

"No, Mother, Benjamin's friends are not trying to destroy me, they are trying to comfort me and help me."

Even then I hoped that you might be regenerated by the work at the furnace, that you might surrender yourself once more to the Magisterium, that you might be faithful to yourself, and that you might maintain the Work.

Yet that night I dreamt that you were searing my breast with the hot breath of the mare you were riding.

112

"MOTHER, I HAVE MADE UP MY MIND—THE day after tomorrow I will say goodbye to you. I am off to England."

Unconsciously, you were telling me that you were leaving the project truncated, the Work unfinished though the Fire had been lit. You were throwing down your rules and your rhythms, disgracing your beauty, and spoiling all my hopes.

"Nothing will stop me from going. I want you to know that."

Twisted in reason, you considered me an obstacle. What efforts I had to make to control myself! I had to fend off with wisdom the taunts like stones you threw at me; upon wisdom depended the future of the project, and your own fate as well. It gave me hope to think that you yourself, refusing to become a victim, might grow angry with your mad chimeras, combat them, and put them to rout.

"Don't worry about that biologist of noble lineage that Abelardo mentioned to you. He's a good friend, I'll see him in England, but that's all."

You could not deny your destiny by changing yourself into some cute little consort or common ordinary child-bearer. With what venom you spewed out those angry chimeras; you had been made feverish by adulation. How they exposed you to putrefaction!

"No, Mother. Nothing is going to sully me, as you put it. You have to understand that children are not the property of their parents."

Your disintegrating soul lost its purest virtues, and corruption prevented you from bringing goodness and knowledge into harmony.

"I owe you thanks for what you did for me, Mother, but I can't spend my entire life as some will-less little doll in your hands."

With what abnegation and what squandering of wealth I had sacrificed my life to you! You had always eclipsed me! Though I never begged for words of praise from you, how humiliated I was by your ravings!

I dreamt that you were riding majestically, on the back of a camel, toward a beautiful garden. You defied the dragon that guarded the entrance. The first swipe of the dragon's paw sent you reeling to the ground, and the fire that issued from its nostrils burned your hands.

113

WITH WHAT VAST AND CUNNING PERFIDY
Benjamin wove his scheme! Drawing upon his renown as
a pianist, he assembled that group of foreign scholars who
came to our land and destroyed your faculty of reason. You
did not just break with the project, you rebelled with fury
against it.

"I want to think for myself, Mother. I want to be free."

You looked at me out of the eyes of a madwoman; your
words were delirium.

"I am not in love with that English nobleman, you can
rest assured of that."

In fits and starts you revealed to me the things that you
had kept inside for so many weeks.

"But we are all going to England with Benjamin and
Abelardo."

Through the uninterrupted gnawing of those materialist maggots, impurity had at last corrupted all your virtues. What profound disillusionment!

"I feel such great affection for Abelardo, Mother. And he feels strongly for me, too. With him, everything is so different! The rest of them are just good friends."

A single cloud, but how dark and lowering it was, covered my entire sky. Betrayal, in that cloud's darkness, had dressed the vault of the heavens in mourning.

"Yes. Abelardo and I are going to live together, forever."

I could not believe that you were going to become a bride of stone. What terrible suffering you caused me!

I dreamt that a seventeenth-century artillery piece shot off a cannonball. The projectile fell into a pond, scaring off the swans. From the place where the shell had exploded, an enchanting young woman emerged. She gazed at her image reflected in the mirror of the water, but she looked at herself for so long and with such blind love that she did not see that a second cannonball was coming directly at her. When the missile struck the beautiful virgin, she was blown to atoms, and then she was transformed into a flower.

114

OUR LAST CONVERSATION BEGAN ON THE
evening of June 8. Twelve hours later you would no longer
be alive. You rebuked me terribly; your humors had become
utterly unbalanced:

"Don't keep insisting, Mother. I'm not going to change
my mind. I am leaving tomorrow for London, and I am
breaking all my ties to you."

Ever faithful to my duty, I tried to breathe a cool breeze
over your soul, to reduce your fever. Truth had to emerge
victorious against the pessimists, the deniers, and the skeptics
who surrounded you. That pack of charlatans had perpe-
trated a confidence scheme against you. How ready they
were to reject as legerdemain or marvel the reality they
could neither teach nor learn. I had to save you. With what
resolve I had warned you that I would prefer you dead than

a traitor to our project. Those dark intrigues had so suborned and corrupted you that you had become a spiritual hetaira.

"There will be no hatred when I say goodbye to you tomorrow, Mother, believe me. Please know that Abelardo will not transform me, as you think he will, into his slave. Quite the contrary, he will allow me to achieve my goals with full freedom and independence."

Such disarrangement of mind, and such a wealth of folly, terrified me. You could not travel to London with the furnace.

"Don't you think, Mother, that there can be more exciting, passionate things in life than being locked up with you every night in the cellar working at the furnace?"

With what cruel rage you blasphemed! A froth of bile spewed from your mouth. The putrefaction could be seen in your funereal and macabre eyes.

I looked at you and I saw your skeleton with its twelve keys. I closed my eyes. I looked at you again and I saw your cadaver, within a transparent sphere, devoured by maggots. I closed my eyes again. Once again I opened them and I saw you as an old, old woman, kneeling at the foot of your own tomb, which bore an inscription that read: "Virtue lies defeated."

115

WITH WHAT SHAME YOU CONFESSED TO ME
who the villain of the piece was, as though you were begging
for forgiveness from the person who had sacrificed everything for you.

"Abelardo and I are going to be married in England."

You could not abandon the project so blithely. How
delighted and with what comfort I had stood and watched,
in wonder, your last manipulations in the cellar. You had
distilled the Philosopher's Mercury away, leaving the pure
Sulfur in the bottom of the retort. How could I have imagined then that only a few days later you would announce
your desertion! How patiently you approached the fourth
degree of Fire. The amalgam dissolved into itself, and the
colors bloomed, one after another, until at last the red shone
through, the "Flower of the Fisherman." The glow increased
as the dryness grew, signaling the perfection of your labors.

Then with serenity and art you cooled the matter, and a crystalline structure burst forth, composed of tiny rubies, infinitely dense and splendid.

How impotent you would become once you were married to Abelardo. You would not be able to carry the project forward to the creation of the Stone.

"I have other concerns, Mother."

I warned you that you had sworn not to reveal those things that Science and the Adepts had judged sensible and prudent to keep secret. You had promised to keep silent about the fruit of your labors. It was only under the veil of symbols that one might be permitted to transmit the knowledge.

"Don't worry, I won't tell anybody that I have spent every night of my life working at a furnace. Who do you think would be interested in such a fact?"

How cynically you stood upon the verge of the abyss of frivolity! You more than anyone knew that the Work achieved perfect harmony through the natural virtues of inorganic bodies mixed with love.

116

ALL THROUGH THE COURSE OF THAT LAST night I tried to pull out the fevered and seditious roots that clutched at your heart. My arguments began to dissolve your chimeras.

"But Mother, I can't turn back now. The train tickets and the passage on the steamship are bought. They've rented a house for us to live in when we get to London."

What a fabric of excuses, and how inappropriate to the execution of your role in the villa. You were the pure theorist. Yours was the unique mission to employ goodness and perseverance to extract from vulgar metals the Sulfur which was the principal foundation of the Work. All of the memorable events of your life had been lived beside the furnace; in London you would find only regret and insipidity.

With what serenity you had already established the difference between the Gold of the Initiates and the precious metal. How expertly you had created the amalgam of Sulfur and Mercury so that you might generate the Philosopher's Egg, imparting to it the vegetative faculty. You could not leave unfinished that phase of the project. Without a shred of doctrinal support you tried to defend the indefensible:

"Nobody is going to prostitute my conscience. Nobody is going to force me to undertake enterprises unworthy of me. I will not be, as you suggest, some vulgar female sold to the first man that passes by. Abelardo is not the dominating creature you imagine him to be. That is why I respect him."

Two nights before, I had dreamt that Energy appeared to you and me, in the guise of a grave and majestic woman. In her left hand she carried a tower, but with her right hand she was strangling a winged serpent. In a cavernous voice she said:

"Philosopher's Mercury receives its splendor from Sulfur, as the Moon receives its light from the Sun."

117

AS THE NIGHT REACHED ITS END YOU BEGAN to listen to me. But how little time remained to me in which to save you!

Comforted by seeing that your attention was once more fixed upon my words, I attempted yet again to make you recognize what your life in England would be, without me. In exchange for a few tattered honors you would betray your very *raison d'être*. How foolish it was to sacrifice the project to such crumbs and ashes. With what infinite love, gratitude, and admiration through so many years of effort had I stood in awe, watching you work, and progress, at the furnace. You could not in a few hours, on some whim, destroy all our hopes.

You wept for the first time, revealing the first secret signs of expiation, as though a torrent of tears, pent up for years, had broken through the dam of your defenses.

"I feel so weak, Mother, so nervous, so excited. I have no strength left to fight, much less to win."

We were sitting in the darkness talking, under the sheltering wing of discernment.

"All day I walk around without any strength, and anybody can bend my will. It's only at night, with you, that I recover my lucidity. You have to free me, Mother."

How happy I had been in my tireless and ceaseless protection of you. Yet when you worked at night in the cellar I felt that you were so superior to me! What care you took when you examined the relationships between the base metallic sulfurs and their respective symbols! What penetration you showed as you established the esoteric order of all experience. I watched you in fascination as you deciphered the Enigma.

"It is you, Mother, who prepared me to carry out the Work, and you who must save me now. Shelter me under the fig tree."

You were referring to the Pharaoh's fig tree which aided and succored the wise in their flight from Egypt, giving them its fruit to nourish them and the cool, limpid wetness of its roots to soothe them.

"Free me, Mother."

What terrible sorrow Benjamin and his band of corrupters, vaunting themselves as scholars, had loosed upon us when they resolved to draw you into their ring.

118

"I LACK THE STRENGTH TO KILL MYSELF, Mother. You who had the courage to bring me into the world have to be strong enough . . . now . . . to . . ."

Quaking in every fiber of my body, I saw that in a veiled way you were exhorting me to end your life.

"It has to be you that does it, Mother. I have failed unforgivably. If I go on living I will leave home and be lost."

Outside the pale of mutual recriminations, we spent the night together, musing aloud. You swung, in terrible agitation, from despair to excitement.

"If I am still alive tomorrow morning I will let myself be drawn in again. I will go to the Hotel Ritz, I will see Benjamin and the English scholars, and everything will begin again. You have to put an end to all this, and it must be tonight."

236 • *The Red Virgin*

We were sitting in the cellar beside the instruments that your decision had emptied of all purpose—the brick furnace, the forceps, the probes, the clay crucibles, the distillation flask, the retorts, and the mortars and pestles. Through so many nights, in that setting, you had performed so many purifications, as long drawn out as they were intricate, in following the meaningful clues toward Animate Mercury!

"Better to die, Mother, than to live in ignominy."

Building an edifice of conjectures and suspicions, so many people imagined, erroneously, that it was I who inspired your final idea—that you should cease to live. How very much your own it was, however!

"For the good of us both, Mother, you have to destroy me. The light of day dazzles and paralyzes my will, and I fall, corrupted and befouled."

A few weeks before, I had dreamt that two female lion-tamers locked your clothes and your books into an iron chest. They put the chest into the fire and heated it to such heat that its compact, solid shape turned into liquid, and then to gas, and then at last shone like a red-hot coal at its hermetic labor.

119

"TOMORROW MORNING, IF I AM STILL ALIVE, I will leave your side forever, and abandon the Work with it. I will be a laughingstock to myself, and the greatest affront to your mission."

I employed all my ingenuity in calculating ways of dissuading you from finding your deliverance in death. But how tenaciously you replied, all throughout the night, to my recommendations and advice. What grievous sufferings I was forced to bear with strength and resignation. Seeing you the mistress of your own will, the absolute monarch of your own actions, and your own folly, I was so reminded of the little girl who had years ago undertaken the Work at the furnace with such imperturbability. You had always been able to raise the fire up to the heavens, like some formal manifestation of its resemblance to its celestial home. How artfully during all your labors did you make of the flame the sign and signature of Fire.

"Kill me, Mother. And have no fear, no one will consider this most courageous act of your life an act of cowardice. Don't hesitate any longer. You must destroy me, this very night."

You choked off my objections, and with no emotion whatsoever you arranged the details of your end:

"I want you to do away with me as I sleep. Don't let me wake up from my dreams!"

It was you who loaded the revolver and placed it in my hand, yours was the idea to take a sleeping draught, and it was your decision to leave no message for Benjamin, or for Abelardo, or for the English dons. As you lay in your bed you begged me:

"When I am asleep, shoot me six times in the temple. Here!"

It took you ten years to extract Gold from Sulfur, and twenty-seven days to draw Mercury from Lead. But the decision to die took you only moments.

120

AT MIDNIGHT, MY HEART RIPPED IN TWO BY pain, I gave in to your demand.

"I don't want to suffer, Mother. I want death to come to me when I'm fast asleep."

It occurred to me that you might still soothe your cares and uproot your dark and mournful sentiments. Working at the furnace, you would find the peace you were seeking.

"No, Mother, you know very well that in order to achieve the Gift, the Treasure of Treasures, one must show at least good works. If I wake up tomorrow morning, I will go to England, and I will never again perform another."

I had followed your last good work, step by step, fascinated, enthralled, enchanted. First you diluted the entire mass of Sulfur in a volume of Water three times greater. Then you decanted the solution, separated the dregs, and subjected the liquor to the slow distillation of the bath. When one could begin to make out the Star and the Flower through the vapors, you recommenced the operations seven times, my admiration for you growing in proportion to the phases, and reaching its zenith when at last you multiplied the Seeds in both quantity and virtue.

When you had taken the sleeping potion, you anxiously asked me:

"You *will* do it, won't you, Mother?"

I massaged the occipital region of your head, and sleep began to dull your mental faculties. But how long it took you to fall asleep! If I stopped brushing my hand across your head, you would open your eyes, hovering between dream and lucidity. With a lump of grief in my throat, I watched you, knowing that I had the terrible but irrecusable duty to obey you.

Your body was much more than your visible covering, than your protective sanctuary. I could not end your life without making an awesome effort, calling upon courage and wisdom, the same virtues that you would use in the cellar to extract, as if it were a dragon locked within a castle, the Philosopher's Stone.

121

EMBRACED BY THE DRUG, YOU AT LAST FELL
into a soft, long, peaceful sleep. I went out onto the terrace
and let the cool night breeze sweep the clouds from my
mind. I made the decision to wait until the first light of
dawn to do what you had asked of me.

I returned to the room where you slept. I examined the
six bullets in the revolver I had bought to protect and succor
you, and which now was going to keep you from going
astray. I knew that my hand could hold it, for your sake,
without trembling.

What heartache I felt as I thought of the end of the
world, of a universal cataclysm that might bring about the
total destruction of the planet and the extermination of all
its inhabitants. My mind was so fuddled that I could accept
as reasonable the idea that after your death you would be

reborn directly from the ground, like some simple vegetable, without prior seed, to renew the human race.

Revolver in hand, I approached the bed where you lay fast asleep. I sat beside you, waiting for morning, when I would obey your dreadful order.

I took refuge in hallucination. To my mind came visions of Noah's Ark after the universal Flood, images of monstrous duels between Fire and Water. Your death did not appear to me in these deliriums as the annihilation of your work but rather as a first act of regeneration. That is why I imagined you being reborn in peace, bathed in the wind of the Age of Gold, standing in brilliance. Those hours I spent awaiting the fateful moment—how eternal they seemed to me!

Paralyzed by grief, I spent the night in mad and foolish thoughts. I imagined volcanoes vomiting forth lava upon the oceans, the earth covered for centuries by total darkness, and tempests of fire consuming the planets. I felt so devastated!

How infinitely more painful it is to murder one's daughter than to give birth to her!

122

AT FOUR O'CLOCK IN THE MORNING, AN hour before sunrise, you were still sleeping, as though you were already half dead.

What unending martyrdom of grief I underwent that night! How afraid I was that I would go mad! What a terrible mission you had charged me with! Nothing could quell the fires of my inward hell. My heart sank, and I felt so helpless!

Seized with hopelessness, I reflected that your project would be aborted, that it would fail upon your death, since all things that lived in it and for it, their due times foreseen and determined, had their center in your labors at the furnace. Even the furnace itself was doomed to perish. And yet with what rigor you had stood beside the furnace and fixed the evolutionary stages, dividing them one from another by fleeting periods of inactivity. I wondered whether the eternity of death might not fade with the renaissance of your work, the rebirth of your life. Your temporal life, no mere convulsion could once and for all cut off.

I felt so cumbersome and ugly, so old and useless, so inharmonious and unstrung within the cycles of temporal plurality. There weighed upon my flesh, my bones, and my soul all the pain and grief of the universe.

Your eyes opened for an instant, and you looked at me with such calm repose.

"You still haven't done it, Mother?"

I kissed your brow for the first and last time. I said to you:

"Sleep in peace, my daughter."

You closed your eyes once more, and seconds later you were fast asleep. I began to hear the sounds of the trash collectors on their rounds. Morning had come.

At the furnace you had changed Mercury into Sulfur, Sulfur into Elixir, and Elixir into the Crown of Wisdom. That triple mutation confirmed how right I had been to impart to you the secret Learning.

After receiving such high reward and emblem, how could you have rebelled, as you did, against your very inspiration?

123

HOW FEARFULLY I APPROACHED YOUR BED when the first light of day appeared. I carried the revolver in my hand.

You were sleeping so profoundly! I aimed at the juncture of the left parietal with the frontal and sphenoid. I squeezed the trigger at point-blank range and fired.

In your skull a tiny hole opened, and your body shook as the life flowed out of it.

Blood bubbled from your mouth. Your lips moved as though they were trying to say something, but your mouth only exhaled a sigh.

I took aim again, a few centimeters from the first wound. I fired another bullet at point-blank range. Your body no longer stirred, or shivered.

Overcome with grief and beside myself with pain, I suddenly feared that your heart was still beating, that a breath of life still remained.

I raised the revolver and took aim at your heart and fired a third time.

Exhausted with suffering, I realized that I had not hit your heart but rather your right lung. The terrible sacrifice had not yet ended.

I fired for the last time, taking aim with infinite precision at the center of your heart. The bullet found its mark.

I fell exhausted, crushed, and in pain. I hurt so terribly that I could not cry.

For a few moments my mind was set on using the two bullets that remained to kill myself, but what a despicable way out that desertion would have been!

Your body, dead, gently bled from the four orifices I had opened.

Oppressed by my anguish, for a few minutes I lost consciousness. I dreamt that a horse loaded with books gave a tremendous kick at the mirror that the Empress, in masculine attire, was carrying. The Empress was riddled by the splinters and shards of the mirror, and as she lay dying she barked and brayed as though she were trying to send me some hermetic message.

124

AN HOUR AFTER YOU DIED, OUT OF MY WITS with grief, I hired the taxi that drove me to the police. To my eyes, how surprised and baffled the inspector seemed!

I was subjected to a brace of medical examinations and countless psychiatric and forensic inspections, until at last I was incarcerated in the Women's Prison.

My trial lasted three days. I related the events to the court precisely as they had occurred. I was forced to manifest my absolute disagreement with the defense attorney, who, in order to avoid other trials and other jurisdictions, sought to have me listed among the ranks of the deranged.

I was condemned to twenty-eight years, eight months, and one day of prison. That sentence, ratifying my guilt, has been my only victory since the day of your death. What did it matter to me whether I lived the rest of my days locked in a prison, if you were no longer with me? I had renounced the world completely. With you I had been so perfectly happy! We had achieved such pure goodness!

Months afterward, during the chaos that attended the beginning of the war, the prison in which I was confined was attacked, its gates broken down, and the inmates freed.

Abelardo came forward from the crowd to greet me, coughing. How touching was his bent and emaciated silhouette among the mob of shouting and gesticulating people that surrounded him!

"I did not, you know, have the courage to visit you either during the trial or while you were imprisoned. Do you know something? . . . So often I have thought I saw your daughter . . . in the street . . . like some wondrous apparition . . . that vanishes when I stub my toe against reality."

How many times had I too, trembling with happiness, thought I saw you once again in the prison, when a new inmate was admitted whose face or figure resembled yours!

"Forgive me for everything. I have done you much harm, and I know it. Allow me to give you this notebook. Your daughter wrote in it secretly. I managed to save it before the villa was searched by the detectives. It belongs to you."

It was your secret notebook, the fragments of your *Inferno*. I opened it at random and read:

"*You, you will ride your steed in the sunlight, but I, I shall crawl beneath the earth.*"

I realized that you had written that message before you died in order to urge me to be happy. Doing somersaults among the stars, my eyes dancing, how joyous I suddenly felt!